Praise for *No Excuses*

Which teenager doesn't dream of becoming a sports star? My idol was the 1960 Olympic decathlon champion, Rafer Johnson. He awakened my ambition to train for all disciplines. Oh dear! Shot and discus were heavy, hurdles high, the sandpit in the pole vaulting quite deep, the 1500m race excruciating. Ultimately, I did not have enough talent to become a "king of athletes." Nevertheless, these were important lessons in developing will and perseverance, and in making friends—according to the recommendation of the prince of poets, Johann Wolfgang von Goethe: "One look into a book and two at life!" In *No Excuses*, Stephen Harris captures that will and perseverance needed to be the very best. A wonderful book.

—Volker Kluge, editor, *Journal of Olympic History*

D0094576

Also by Stephen L. Harris

100 Golden Olympians

Duty, Honor, Privilege: *New York's Silk Stocking Regiment and the Breaking of the Hindenburg Line*

Harlem's Hell Fighters: *The African-American 369th Infantry in World War I*

Duffy's War: *Fr. Francis Duffy, Wild Bill Donovan, and the Irish Fighting 69th in World War I*

Rock of the Marne: *The American Soldiers Who Turned the Tide Against the Kaiser in World War I*

NO EXCUSES

By Stephen L. Harris

Rootstock Publishing

Montpelier, VT

Release Date: August 2, 2022
First Printing: 2022

No Excuses

Softcover ISBN: 978-1-57869-094-7
Hardcover ISBN: 978-1-57869-095-4
eBook ISBN: 978-1-57869-096-1
Library of Congress Control Number: 2022901592

Cover design by Eddie Vincent

Author photo by Mark Harris

Book design by Tim Newcomb

For permissions or to schedule an author interview, contact the author
at slharris@gmavt.net.

Published by Rootstock Publishing,
an imprint of Multicultural Media, Inc.
Montpelier, Vermont
www.rootstockpublishing.com
info@rootstockpublishing.com

Printed in the USA

To my son, Mark, a wonderful decathlete,
who showed me the way.

Author's Note

The inspiration for *No Excuses* was my son, Mark. Watching him compete in track and field in high school and college, seeing his grace and determination, overcoming adversity, and never giving up, taught me a lot, even as a parent. His best events were the high hurdles and pole vault. He was Connecticut's state pole vault champion, both indoor and outdoor, and set numerous records. He also won the New England Intercollegiate Decathlon Championship back in the early 1990s.

As I watched him perform, I thought what a wonderful book the history of the Olympic decathlon would make. I set out to research the book, tracking down long-ago competitors as well as current stars. I met and interviewed a number of Olympians and became friends with 1968 gold medalist Bill Toomey from New Canaan, Connecticut, a New York City suburb next to Wilton, the town where I grew up. Through Bill, I made connections to the United States Olympic Committee. In 1996, I was hired to write *100 Golden Olympians* for the USOC to honor America's greatest living champions on the eve of the hundredth anniversary of the modern Olympics, first held in Athens, Greece, in 1896.

I interviewed almost all the great Olympians, including my childhood hero Bob Mathias, who won the decathlon gold medal twice—in 1948, when he became the youngest track-and-field champion in Olympic history, and again in 1952. Jeff Blatnick, the Greco-Roman victor who had to win his battle with cancer before taking on the world's best wrestlers. High jumper Alice Coachman, who in 1948 became the first Black woman to win a gold medal. Hurdler and sprinter Harrison Dillard, nicknamed "Bones," who, after being inspired by the great Jesse Owens, captured gold medals in 1948 and 1952. And hockey star Mike Eruzione, who captained the famous U.S. Olympic men's hockey team to a stunning win in the Miracle on Ice game in 1980.

But one of the stars who most inspired me to write this book was Glenn Davis, gold medalist in the intermediate hurdles in 1956 and 1960, who also ran a leg of the 4x100 relay for his third gold medal. When he was a teenager, both his parents died on the same day. Heartbroken, Glenn had a hard time adjusting and was headed down life's dead-end street. Angry at the world, he took aggression out on the football field and the track. With his motto "No Excuses," he set world records in the 400 meters and the hurdles at Ohio State University, made the U.S. Olympic team, and scored his most thrilling victories in Australia and Rome. In 1996, I wrote his life story titled, of course, "No Excuses."

Another golden Olympian I interviewed back then was Bruce Jenner, known today as Caitlyn after bravely coming out as a woman. In this book I refer to her as Bruce because my story takes place in the 1980s, before there was a Caitlyn Jenner. I trust everyone understands.

There are a number of people I need to thank for their gracious help with this book—either inspirationally or hands on. My son Mark, of course. My wife of many years, Sue, who is always by my side. My grandson, Connor, just starting out in this brave new world. Bill Toomey; Glenn Davis, who alas has since passed; David Wallechinsky, extraordinary Olympic historian and former president of the International Society of Olympic Historians; my agent, Judy Coppage; and my innovative publisher at Rootstock, Stephen McArthur, sharp-eyed copyeditor Sheryl Rapée-Adams, and proofreader Marisa Keller.

1

On an early spring day many years ago, in the time of no cell phones, Skeets Stearns, clad only in a torn bathing suit in spite of the cold weather, raced along the edge of a cliff in a lonesome corner of northeastern Vermont. Like a mountain lion, he jumped over boulders and fallen trees. In his right hand he clutched a long, sturdy pole, cut from a sapling. He used it to vault boulders too high to jump. As he ran he saw the valley far below. He saw the shiny blacktop of the road like a snake slithering across the valley floor. He saw the village of Hackett's Falls. He saw his parents' small farmhouse, like a smudge at the bottom of the mountain.

If any of the villagers were to see him sprinting atop Catamount Ridge—especially Emile McIntosh, the big bully who loved to torment him and others like him with noogies, those scalp-burning knuckle rubs, in front of his high school classmates—they'd be shocked. That meant red-haired Becky Winslow, too, with her splash of tiny freckles across a pretty face, who'd stolen his heart but had yet to give him the time of day. Yes, she'd be shocked if she could see him now.

Resting a moment on an outcropping of granite, Skeets felt his heart pound inside his chest. He was the last of the great pumas. He gulped in the high mountain air, certain there was no feeling like it in the whole world. Raising his arms above his head—his long dark hair, worn like the Indians who used to roam the forest, dangling against his bare shoulders—he let go a frenzied whoop. He listened to it echo across the valley to where the Green Mountains rose up again to continue their geologic march north into Quebec, Canada. If there was a heaven this was it!

In the distance, the deep blue waters of Lake Memphremagog shone like a mirror in the late afternoon sun. Skeets and his father and Uncle Jacques, on his mother's side, a retired navy bosun's mate, part French Canadian, part Abenaki Indian, and no bigger than Skeets himself, fished the lake for largemouth bass. From their outboard motorboat they could look back and see Catamount Ridge, a gray cliff scarring its side.

"Are mountain lions really up there?" Skeets always asked when they were out on Memphremagog. The legend of a mountain lion on Catamount Ridge was as strong as the legend of Scotland's Nessie, the monster of Loch Ness, or Champ, the monster of nearby Lake Champlain.

"Well if there is, I've never seen one," was his father's constant reply. He was a practical man with a practical man's outlook on life. Farming land pocked with rocks was the only way he knew. His calloused hands proved it. To him, it wasn't practical for lions to be roaming the Green Mountains. Any fool knew they'd been hunted into extinction years ago, same as wolves and northern caribou. But Uncle Jacques, who knew the forest better than anyone in Vermont's Northeast Kingdom and who had sailed around the world aboard the USS *Independent*, one of the largest aircraft carriers ever, always winked at Skeets and smiled as if he knew something his brother-in-law didn't.

Skeets began to run again. Effortlessly, he moved along the ridge. Maybe someday he'd see a mountain lion. He'd seen plenty of deer and black bear, and in a bog halfway down the mountain he'd once seen an old bull moose, its antlers as broad as an eagle's wings. Skeets jumped a log. He dodged a boulder. He planted the pole and vaulted to the top of a huge rock. His small, muscled body bubbled with sweat. Behind him the sun was sinking low in the sky. It was time to head home.

Using the pole, he swung off the rock. He loped away from the edge of the cliff and into the dark shadows of the forest. It was cool among the trees. He found an animal path and followed its switchback pattern down the side of Catamount Ridge until he came to a river. Two deer drinking at the river's edge looked up. Skeets skidded to a stop. The eyes of the deer were as black as coal. The larger of the two snorted and then both deer bolted into the underbrush and were gone. No matter how many times he saw deer he always got excited. He never hunted them like his father and Uncle Jacques, a pair of veteran hunters, although they kept encouraging him to take up a rifle and follow them into the woods.

Skeets resumed his run down the mountain. But this time he took to the river. The water was cold and crusted with ice. The riverbed was sandy. Uprooted by storms, thick trees were strewn across the river, making natural bridges and dams. Where the river rushed against the fallen timber, pools formed. Sometimes the pools were over Skeets's head and he had to swim. Sometimes he dove under the trunks of sunken trees, weaving in and out of the branches like the otter, now imagining himself an otter. Sometimes he scrambled over them like a monkey, now imagining himself a monkey swinging free.

At a heavily wooded place halfway down the mountain, the roar of white water was deafening. Here the river cascaded into a deep gorge. To keep from being swept over the cascade, Skeets left the river and climbed onto a rocky overhang. The force of the river had carved out a corkscrew cave on the steep north wall of the gorge. The cave didn't lead anywhere, but it was a perfect hiding spot. It surprised Skeets that no one knew about this wonderful place—not even Uncle Jacques. But he was glad. His heart thumped more from joy than exertion. The gorge was his secret place, belonging only to him. He knew every inch of it the way his father knew every inch of the family cornfield.

Skeets hurled his pole like a javelin. It sailed across the gorge and into the mouth of the cave. The sound of its hitting the mark was silenced by the river's roar. When he knew his throw was true, Skeets jumped. He tucked his knees under his chin and grabbed them, cannonball style. And like a cannonball he plunged into the frigid pool at the bottom of the waterfall, and sank to its darkest depths.

The strong current held Skeets under, as if the river was scolding him for invading this place. But then it let go and pushed him to the edge of the pool. He surfaced, gasping. Digging his fingers and toes into the granite wall, he climbed up to the cave. Inside, his clothes were in a heap. He put them on. Once his sneakers were tightened and tied, he scrambled out of the cave and scaled the last bit of wall to the top of the gorge. He looked across to where he'd cannonballed into the river. It was a good fifty-foot drop. He then turned and, like the legendary catamount of olden times, vanished into the gloom of the forest.

2

When Skeets slipped out of the woods, breathing heavily from the run down the mountain, the long shadow of Catamount Ridge was already over the farm where he lived, and it was like evening. His father had named the farm Hard Scrabble. It was a house and a barn on twenty acres of rocky land. The house was a tired old structure that tilted away from the foot of the mountain as if something fearful lurked among the trees. Even the barn was old and tired. It needed paint and a new roof. The farm's only sign of hope was the freshly plowed cornfield next to the barn and the rutted path the cows followed to get to their pasture.

Walking across the yard, Skeets sensed something wasn't right. Parked next to his father's pickup truck was a strange station wagon. The license plate wasn't Vermont green. It was New York blue and white. He wondered who the car might belong to. His family rarely had out-of-state visitors. He tiptoed onto the porch and peered through the window. His parents were at the kitchen table sipping coffee. Across from them was a stranger. The stranger had long hair pulled back into a ponytail. Skeets figured him to be in his late forties, maybe early fifties. He wore a flannel shirt and jeans and hiking boots. He sat at the table with a certain athletic grace that Skeets noticed right away. Although the stranger was only slightly bigger than Skeets's father, he dwarfed his mother. But that wasn't unusual. His mother was dwarfed by everyone—except Uncle Jacques, her brother. Skeets was certain he'd inherited her family genes and was doomed to be small, too. Taking a deep breath, he entered the house.

Mrs. Stearns beamed. "This is our son, Skeets, we've been telling you about," she said.

The stranger smiled and stood up. He had a tired face and the lines in it were deeply etched. There was a weary sadness in his eyes, too, that told Skeets he'd lived a life as hard as any farmer. Skeets measured him to be at least six feet tall, maybe taller. Skeets reached across the table, looking for a handshake. The stranger offered him his left hand, not his right. The right hung limply at his side. Skeets grasped the stranger's left hand. It felt unnatural for shaking, but he shook it anyway. He felt it was the right thing to do.

"This is Mr. MacColl," his mother said. "He and your uncle Jacques served in the navy together way before you were born. His mother recently passed on, so he's come up here all the way from New York City to experience country life."

"Call me Bill," the stranger said.

"How ya do?" said Skeets, looking at his mother for some clue as to why the stranger was there, in his house. *To experience country life?* To Skeets it sounded like he'd already moved in.

"Mr. MacColl's going to live with us for a bit," she said. "It was your uncle Jacques's idea."

So he was right. He let go of the stranger's hand. He turned to his father and then back to his mother. They knew their farmhouse had only two bedrooms. One was his, and he wasn't going to share it with anyone—particularly a one-armed man. "But there's no place for him to stay!"

"Mr. MacColl will soon live in the barn," his father said, sounding as practical as ever.

Any fool knew barns were for animals. "Why there's nuthin' out there 'cept cows," Skeets said. "And an old empty horse stall!"

Mr. MacColl smiled. "I'm born and raised in Gotham—in New York City, that is. Now that my mother's gone, I need to get away for a while. Live in the country so I can partake of Vermont's pristine Green Mountains before they're gone."

Partake? "But in the barn?" Skeets asked.

"We're going to fix up the horse stall for Mr. MacColl so he can live there," Mr. Stearns said. "It'll take a few weeks, maybe more, to do the work. So we've offered Mr. MacColl your room till we're finished. We know you won't mind sleeping on the living room couch."

"I'm not giving up my room," Skeets said.

"I can sleep on the couch," Mr. MacColl said quickly. "I don't want to be a bother."

"You'll be no bother," Mrs. Stearns said. "And I'm disappointed in you, Skeets. I thought you had better manners than that. You should be happy to offer your room to Mr. MacColl. It's only for a few weeks."

"Nobody wants to live in a horse stall that's never lost its smell! I'll be sleeping on that old couch the whole time!"

Skeets looked at the stranger. *Why was he here in the first place?* It was weird business as far as he was concerned. Maybe the mother's death had nothing to do with it. Maybe Mr. MacColl was an outlaw on the run, even if he knew Uncle Jacques and they'd been in the navy together. Yeah, that was it. Maybe he'd been shot in the arm. Maybe that's why it was a useless piece of flesh and bone. Maybe he had to hide out until his arm got better. He looked for dried blood on the sleeve of the flannel shirt. A sure telltale sign that he was on the run. There wasn't any.

"Well, I hope you ain't a gangster on the lam." The words just tumbled out of his mouth. His cheeks burned red. But he was darned if he'd put up with an intruder.

"Skeets!" his mother said.

Skeets bolted from the kitchen. Outside, a cold wind swept down the mountainside. He didn't like the idea of someone moving in with him—in with his family—and kicking him out of *his* room. Crossing the yard to the old barn, he heard the cows moving about. He smelled them, strong as ever. Jeezum crow, why the dickens would anyone want to live in such a smelly place? Something wasn't right. He'd keep an eye on this Mr. William MacColl. He'd better tell Emile McIntosh about him, that's for sure—even if he got his head locked inside Emile's thick arms and suffered one of his embarrassing noogies that burned his scalp raw while Becky Winslow sometimes looked on, shaking her head as if to ask "Why don't you fight back?" Skeets shrugged off that vision. Anyway, Emile would know what to do. Yeah, he was big enough to take care of this Mr. MacColl. He scooped up a rock and chucked it as far as he could into the cornfield, cursing his uncle Jacques for his dumb idea.

"I'm not giving up my room to anyone," he muttered.

3

That night around the kitchen table Skeets ate in silence while listening to the conversation between Mr. MacColl and his parents. His mother had made his favorite meal, pork chops and applesauce, mashed potatoes, and a garden salad. He reckoned she did it because she knew he was angry since he had to give up his room, even for a few weeks. They talked mostly about New York City, a place no one in the family had been except Uncle Jacques.

"I've been to Boston once," Mr. Stearns said. "I went down with my brother-in-law to see the Red Sox play the Yankees. You must be a Yankee fan, coming from New York."

"Actually, I'm a Mets fan," Mr. MacColl answered. "Because of my father. He loved the Dodgers back in the fifties when they were still in Brooklyn, before they moved out to LA. He'd tell me stories about their games against the old New York Giants and their subway series with the Yankees. Great players in those days. Pee Wee Reese at short, Jackie Robinson at second, Duke Snider holding down center field, and Carl Furillo, the Reading Rifle, in right. The Giants had Willie Mays in center. The other great center fielder in New York back then was Mickey Mantle. Can you imagine a single city with three of the greatest center fielders ever all playing at the same time—Mays, Mantle, and Snider? Truly amazing."

With the use of only one arm, he ate with the dexterity of a man with two good arms. He kept switching back and forth between knife and fork, fork and knife. He did it with such speed that even Skeets had to admire him. But he still didn't have to like him.

"I could never warm to the Yankees," Mr. MacColl went on. "They win all the time. Now the Mets—the Miracle Mets—are finally giving them a run for their money." He took a bite of pork chop. "You know, Jackie Robinson broke the major league color

8

line in 1947, playing with the old Dodgers. He was one of the best infielders ever."

"Better than Wade Boggs of my Red Sox?" Skeets said.

"You bet. I know of Wade Boggs. He's still early in his career, but he'll never be as good as Robinson," Mr. MacColl answered.

"How come I never heard of this Jackie Robinson?" a skeptical Skeets said.

"Probably because you're too young."

"I heard of him plenty," piped up Mr. Stearns. "I remember seeing a newsreel of him stealing home in the World Series against the Yankees. Now, that was something!"

"Well," Mr. MacColl said, "when the Dodgers and Giants gave up New York for California in 1958 it left a big baseball void in the Big Apple, until my Mets came along in 1962, with their spanking new uniforms sporting Dodger blue and Giant orange as a reminder of the good old days. My old man's stories were great and I loved them. Made me love sports history. It also made me a big Mets fan, a National Leaguer all the way."

"What's New York like?" Skeets's mother asked, changing the subject.

Mr. MacColl shrugged. "I guess it's like any other place, except bigger. Everything's bigger in New York. And faster, too."

"That's why they call it the Big Apple," Skeets said with a touch of sarcasm, then went back to poking at his meal.

"But in neighborhoods like Greenwich Village, where I grew up, there's actually a small-town atmosphere. A lot like here in Hackett's Falls, I bet."

"I can hardly believe that," said Mrs. Stearns. "What's it really like living in such a big city?"

"It can be claustrophobic, that's for sure," Mr. MacColl said. "What with towering skyscrapers that block out the sun. Unlike up here in Vermont where there's so much open space. You feel freer, I bet."

"Oh, I don't know about that," said Mr. Stearns. "Farming keeps you pretty much tied to the land."

"I don't know much about farming. My parents ran a bookstore. I went to New York University a few blocks from where I lived.

I'd hang out at Washington Square and listen to folk singers like Bob Dylan and Joan Baez and watch old men sit around and play checkers or chess. It seems I never went anywhere. Stayed basically on the same block, it seemed, forever."

"That's hard to believe," said Skeets's mother.

"It's true. I joined the navy because of its motto. Join the navy and see the world."

"Why, that's exactly how come my brother Jacques joined the navy," said Mrs. Stearns, nodding knowingly. "To see the world."

"Jacques and I were shipmates aboard the USS *Independent* out of the Seventh Fleet in San Diego. I loved the name of the carrier, *Independent,* a symbol of freedom. During the Vietnam War, we were sent to the Gulf of Tonkin. We jokingly called the Seventh Fleet, when we were there, the Tonkin Yacht Club. I was a bomber pilot and Jacques was my mechanic."

Bomber pilot! Now Mr. MacColl had Skeets's attention.

"Your uncle Jacques," Mr. MacColl said, nodding toward Skeets, "he was always talking about the Green Mountains and said I ought to see them at least once in my life. Well, here I am."

Skeets thought, *Well, you've seen them. Now will you go home?*

"We are sorry to hear that your mom has passed on," Mrs. Stearns said.

"Yes, we are so sorry," added Mr. Stearns.

"Thank you," Mr. MacColl said. "We lived together in the same old brownstone where I grew up. One of these days I'll have to go back and clean it out and put it on the market. I don't think I can bear it. It's been my home for as long as I can remember."

"Is your dad gone, too?"

"He died of a heart attack while I was overseas in the navy. I—I . . ."

Why did Mr. MacColl not finish what he started to say? Skeets sensed that maybe he had wanted to confess a dark family secret. But he closed up instead, and said no more.

When it was bedtime, Skeets's mother pulled out the sofa bed in the living room and made it up. Because there was only one bathroom, it took some time before everyone was ready for bed.

Another annoyance! Skeets climbed onto the couch and flicked off the light. He was too upset to go to sleep. Tonight he'd not dream of Becky Winslow and her red hair and freckles and that smile of hers that always made his heart thump a little more, especially whenever she laughed. Instead, he stared into the dark and listened. He listened to Mr. MacColl go into *his* room. Then he heard him pace back and forth, the floorboards squeaking with each step.

Why? thought Skeets, still staring into the dark and listening.

4

ill MacColl stopped pacing. He lay back on Skeets's bed and did not move, the good arm resting on his forehead, the bad arm dangling to the floor, useless as a fishing line without bait. The only way he moved that arm was to grab it with his good hand and put it where he wanted. Shadows flickered on the walls of the room. Near midnight, he looked at his watch and then counted the seconds until both hands touched twelve. When the second hand crossed over into morning, he smiled and silently wished himself a happy birthday.

He was now forty years old. The big four-oh! No one knew it was his birthday and so there was no one to share it with. It was better that way, he thought.

Closing his eyes with no intention to sleep, he drew out of the deepest recesses of his mind that moment in 1968 when, on a bombing mission, his jet had been shot out of the skies over the steamy jungles of Vietnam, thudded into the side of a mountain, and exploded into a fiery ball of flames and black smoke. His parachute had partially opened when he bailed out and he crashed into the thick, vine-covered trees. Branches snapped as he pitched toward the ground, landing hard on his side. The pain in his leg and arm forced him to cry out. The Vietcong, an enemy clad in black, was nearby and would be on him soon. With his working hand, he pulled his knife from its sheath, cut himself free from the parachute, and then somehow, using all his strength, crawled off into the tangled underbrush, dragging the parachute with him. He kept crawling in spite of the intense pain, biting his lip to keep from crying out. When he'd gone a fair distance he pulled himself up into a tree. He climbed to the topmost branches, trying to hide among the green leaves and twisted vines. He snapped off a twig, clamped his teeth around it, and bit down hard so he'd keep quiet and not give himself away.

Bill MacColl was twenty-three then, a second lieutenant just commissioned in the navy as a bomber pilot, and engaged to marry Kathleen Fleming, his college sweetheart. He'd enlisted in the navy while in college for two reasons. First, because he thought it was his duty to serve his country while it was at war in Southeast Asia. Second, because he wanted to see the world. Kathleen had begged him not to go—fearing something terrible might happen to him. While at New York University he'd been a student officer in the Reserve Officers Training Corps, the ROTC, but more importantly, the star of the university's track-and-field team—a great decathlete with a chance to make it to the Olympics in Mexico City in 1968, the year he'd hoped to graduate from college and get a military deferment until after the Olympics. Then he'd willingly fulfill his obligation. The deferment never came. Instead, he found himself stationed with the Seventh Fleet in the Gulf of Tonkin off the Vietnam coast.

It was his first mission, roaring off the aircraft carrier USS *Independent* in the dark of night to bomb roads and bridges along the Ho Chi Minh Trail that wound through dense jungle, carrying supplies to the enemy. It was somewhere in the jungle that his bomber was shot down by a surface-to-air missile. He'd ejected and parachuted down, crashing through trees and vines and thick vegetation.

* * *

He'd never been in a jungle before, up in the mountains. The vegetation was thick and close around him. Blood flowed from a head wound. When he first tried to stand he discovered he had a useless right arm and no feeling in his right leg, though the pain coursed through every other part of his body. He couldn't see the starry night sky through the smoke and thickly leafed treetops. Darkness was all around him. His breathing became heavy. He felt claustrophobic. His biggest fear was that he might be found, captured by the Vietcong. Hiding among the branches of the tree, he prayed he'd soon be rescued by his fellow shipmates from the Independent.

At first he could stand the pain. But now it shot through his entire body. Hours passed. The sun rose. Then, below him, he heard voices and the clinking of weapons. Turning his head as best he could, he looked down through the branches and vines. A handful of Vietcong were holding his parachute. One of them was directly beneath him. The man was eerie in his pajama-like black uniform and wide-brimmed hat known as a coolie, a machine gun slung over his shoulder. As the coolie bobbed below him, it mesmerized MacColl. His eyes locked on a single red spot on the coolie. Suddenly, he saw double. Or thought he saw double. There were two red spots— then three! And four! The red was blood—his blood. And it was dripping onto the coolie.

He knew if the rebel heard the spattering of blood against his coolie, or looked up, he was a goner. Holding his breath, he willed himself to stop bleeding. But, like a leaky faucet, blood from his wound continued to drip onto the coolie. For a horribly long time— minutes, hours, an eternity—the Vietcong stood below MacColl. The enemy had to hear it! Had to feel it! Had to smell it! At last one of his comrades called out, and the Vietcong, tossing his parachute on the ground at the base of the tree, melted away into the forest.

Pain engulfed MacColl like an unbearable heat. When he could no longer stand it he drifted off into a dreamy unconsciousness. For the next week he hung in that tree until a rescue helicopter, after spotting the parachute, hovered above the site and found him among the branches, almost dead from shock and loss of blood.

* * *

Since then, he'd never ventured near a forest again.

Returning to the present, Mr. MacColl opened his eyes. He stared up through the gloom of Skeets's room. Sweat dampened his face as if in a fever. He sat up and fumbled across the room to his suitcase. In a moment, he found the whiskey bottle and shot glass. It felt reassuring in his good hand. He uncapped the bottle and poured a shot. He held up the glass and toasted himself. He downed the shot and poured another.

"Here's to Kathleen," he whispered in the dark, "married to another man and a mother now. Here's to my one true love who broke my heart forever."

He emptied the glass. The taste of whiskey was sharp against his tongue. It burned his throat. He coughed, recapped the bottle, and placed it back in the suitcase. After this bottle, he'd quit drinking. This time he meant it. There'd be no excuses. And by then he'd have plenty of nerve to go into the forest that covered Catamount Ridge, as dark and thick as any Vietnam jungle, and throw off the past that still haunted him. Be done with his wounds. Done with his claustrophobia. And get on with his life, at last.

Like his old friend, mentor, and lifelong inspiration, Glenn Davis, the great Olympic hurdler, had said to him in the navy hospital in San Diego while he was recovering from his wounds, "No excuses, Billy. No excuses!"

5

The next morning, while it was still dark out, Skeets came into the kitchen rubbing the sleep from his eyes. His mother was bent over the stove. Steam curled upward, and the sound and smell of bacon and scrambled eggs frying in a pan were a delight to his senses. Outside, his father tended to his chores. Skeets slumped onto his chair. He saw the breakfast table set for four—instead of the usual settings for just him and his parents. Then he remembered the stranger who'd commandeered his bedroom and had spent half the night pacing about.

"Where's Mr. MacColl?" Maybe he'd left.

"He's helping your father." Mrs. Stearns scooped a mound of food onto Skeets's plate.

The door opened and Mr. Stearns and the stranger burst into the kitchen. They were laughing.

"That's a good one," said Mr. Stearns. He looked quickly at his wife as his face reddened. "Just a wee joke," he said.

"Sorry, ma'am," Mr. MacColl said. He winked at Skeets, his eyes blood red and so very weary looking, then joined him at the table.

Skeets slid away from him. Mrs. Stearns put two plates filled with scrambled eggs, bacon, and buttered toast on the table, one for her son and the other for Mr. MacColl. She added two more heaping plates for her husband and herself. Mr. Stearns dug in first, shoveling a forkful of eggs into his mouth. Mr. MacColl reached for a piece of toast. Using the fingers of his good hand, he snapped the toast in two. He leaned the larger of the two pieces against his plate. The smaller one he used to scoop up some of the scrambled eggs.

"Do you play any sports?" he asked Skeets.

"No."

Mr. MacColl bit into his toast and eggs.

"He's got too many chores around the farm to waste time on sports," Mr. Stearns said.

That wasn't it, and Skeets knew it. He was just too small. Too small for football. Too small for basketball. Too small for baseball. When he went out for the school baseball team, the other players scoffed at him, including Emile McIntosh, the biggest and roughest kid in school. Ashamed, Skeets never again went out for a team.

"I'm no good at sports, anyway," he said. Keeping his eyes on his plate, he attacked his eggs.

Mr. MacColl, sensing he'd hit a sore subject with the boy, kept quiet.

"Looks like it'll be a nice day," Mrs. Stearns said. From the window over the sink she could see the backyard and Catamount Ridge. In the morning the sun rose in front of the ridge, splashing its many trees with golden light. She sat down to enjoy her breakfast.

"Well, time to get back to work and for you to go to school." Mr. Stearns stood. Skeets nodded and dashed out of the house. He trotted along the dirt lane that led from his parents' house to the road. Hackett's Falls Regional High School was a mile away, just a short jog.

As soon as he got to school, Skeets ran up to Emile McIntosh. Wearing a Boston Red Sox baseball cap, he was flirting with red-haired Becky Winslow and some other girls. Skeets felt nervous that he'd get another noogie in front of Becky. A senior, Emile played center on the football team and the basketball team, and tossed the shot put and threw the discus and javelin on the track team. He towered over everyone. They called him "Mac" or "the Big Apple."

"Emile, I gotta talk to you," Skeets said. He always called him Emile, mostly out of fearful respect. He glanced at Becky. He remembered she was an athlete like Emile, a star on the girls' track-and-field team. A runner and jumper. For a moment their eyes met and he felt flushed and turned away. *Why was he always shy around Becky?*

Emile lumbered into the cafeteria, Becky and the girls following him. The big boy dumped his books onto one of the long tables

17

where the students ate their lunch. Folding his massive arms over his chest, he looked down at Skeets. "About what?"

"We gotta stranger livin' at our house. In my room. I gotta sleep on the couch!"

"So what?"

"Well, I don't want him sleeping in my room. Besides, he wants to move into the barn. Don't you think that's odd? I mean, livin' in the barn?"

"Next to the cows?" sneered Emile. "I bet he's got cow dung for brains." Emile laughed. The girls all laughed, except Becky. Skeets felt his cheeks burning again.

"Well, my dad and I are gonna fix up one of the horse stalls. Make it into a room for him to live in, with a cot and table and woodstove and everything. He's got a bad arm and walks with a limp."

"He's still got cow dung for brains," Emile said.

A bell rang. Emile scooped up his books. He and Becky walked out of the cafeteria. Skeets tagged along.

"Well, what should I do?" Skeets asked.

"Meet me after practice this afternoon and I'll come over to your place and take a look at this cripple." Emile swaggered down the hallway to his homeroom, students getting out of his way. Skeets watched him with envy. If only he was half Emile's size or had just an ounce of his strength, he'd play sports, too. For a second he saw himself scoring touchdowns or drilling jump shots from far away. And Becky would be admiring his athletic grace. He followed Emile and the girls to their homeroom.

At the door, Becky turned. "Hi, Skeets."

Skeets turned red.

That afternoon, Skeets sat in the bleachers and watched the boys' and girls' track teams practice together. It was better than a three-ring circus. Everywhere were boys, about twenty-five of them, running, jumping, and throwing. At one end of the field, Emile and two others heaved the twelve-pound shot. They grunted loudly with each toss. Emile threw the farthest. At the other end, five or six boys high-jumped. Like the deer in the forest above

Skeets's house, they pranced up to the crossbar. Then they flipped over it, arching their backs as if somebody had lit a match to their rear ends. In front of Skeets, several boys practiced the pole vault. One of them was the likable Tommy Patneau, a farm boy like Skeets. They sprinted down a runway, jammed their poles into a V-shaped box, then sprang upside down as the pole bent backward and shot them skyward. They tumbled onto a big blue mat. Also on the track in front of Skeets, a boy named Billy Abbott jumped over hurdles.

Everywhere he saw girls, too, running, some fast, some slow. Round and round the track they went. He'd never seen a sport where so much went on at one time, and all of it so different. *Yes, like a three-ring circus!*

He especially kept his eyes on one girl. Becky Winslow. She practiced sprints, charging out of the starting blocks and streaking up the track for about twenty yards. Over and over again. When she finished she went over to the long jump pit, measured her steps, ran down the runway, and sprang into the air. Again, over and over.

The afternoon shot past and soon he and Emile were walking home. As they hiked up the long dirt driveway to the farmhouse, they spotted Mr. MacColl as he came out of the barn.

"There he is," Skeets said, nudging Emile's arm. He saw that Mr. MacColl was not as big as Emile.

Mr. MacColl looked at the boys. He stopped and waited for them.

"This is Emile McIntosh," Skeets said.

Mr. MacColl stuck out his left hand. Emile reached for it with his right and then quickly switched to his left as if he'd hardly noticed Mr. MacColl was crippled. As they shook hands, Skeets said, "Emile's our star athlete. He does everything. Football, basketball, and track."

Emile squeezed Mr. MacColl's hand to show him that, even if he was a teenager, he was still a force to reckon with.

Ignoring the powerful grip, Mr. MacColl smiled at Emile and said, "Track." The tone of his voice surprised Skeets, like he

19

actually liked track. "What are your events?"

"The shot put, disc, and jav, but the shot's my best event," said Emile.

"How far can you toss the shot?"

"He's the county champ!" Skeets boasted.

"I've done forty-nine feet," Emile said. "I plan to do better this spring and set the school record of fifty-one feet, and win the state championship."

Mr. MacColl looked at the ground for a moment, searching for something, then bent over and picked up a stone about the size of a shot. "Let me see you toss this rock."

Looking proud to show off his style, Emile grabbed the rock. He hefted it over his head a few times. He placed it snugly on his right shoulder, just behind his ear. He then crouched, holding his left leg up for balance. In a flash he sprang forward and with a loud grunt heaved the rock high and far. They all watched the rock hit the earth in a cloud of dust.

"I wish I was strong enough to throw the shot like that," Skeets said.

Mr. MacColl looked at Skeets for a second. Turning to Emile, he asked, "How far do you think you've got to toss the shot to be state champion?"

"More than fifty feet, that's for sure," Emile said. "There's a kid from Burlington might give me trouble."

"What's your coach think?"

"Well, Coach Norton thinks I can break the school record. Maybe even throw the shot fifty-three feet. I know I can!"

"Coach Norton is really the baseball coach," Skeets said. "But he coaches everything. Football and basketball."

"But Coach Norton doesn't know much about track stuff," Emile said. "Our high school is so small it can afford only one coach. And that's Coach Norton. He teaches shop, too."

Mr. MacColl nodded at this bit of information. He rubbed the back of his neck. "To get better in the shot you've got to be quicker," he said to Emile. "You have the strength. Now you need the speed." He looked at Skeets. "And there's no reason you can't throw the shot either."

"Me?"

"You bet," said Mr. MacColl. "Now, if you boys will excuse me, I've got something to do." He nodded, then limped away.

As soon as he disappeared, Emile scratched his head. "Coach Norton never told me about speed. He just showed me how to hold the shot and crouch and stuff like that. He never said a thing about speed."

"Do you think I could throw the shot?" Skeets asked.

"It's kinda heavy and you're kinda small," Emile said. He turned to go home.

"Yeah," Skeets sighed, "I guess you're right."

Emile looked back. "Yeah, you know I'm right. And that guy's still got cow dung for brains, 'cause he don't know jack about puttin' the shot."

6

*A*nother night on the couch. Skeets wondered when his father would start to convert the stall into a bedroom.

Later that morning he spotted Mr. MacColl lacing up his hiking boots. The stranger sat on a granite boulder outside the barn. Skeets and his father had rolled it there from the cornfield. It took them a full day to move it fifty feet, sweating, grunting, and cursing the old stone the whole way. Skeets marveled at the way Mr. MacColl could lace his boots so quickly with one hand. Mr. MacColl looked up.

"On such a beautiful day as this, I'm hiking up onto the mountain," he said. He tilted his head toward Catamount Ridge.

Skeets felt a jolt sweep through his body. *First my room. Now my mountain.* "You don't wanna go up there," he said, afraid Mr. MacColl might find his secret pool. "There's nuthin' but ticks and deerflies thick as clouds."

Poking a finger into one of his shirt pockets, Mr. MacColl pulled out a small canister. "Bug repellent."

"Well, there's no real trails or anything. Just plenty of prickers and poison ivy and poison oak. You'll get all scratched up, and itch like crazy for weeks."

"Sounds like you're afraid of the forest," Mr. MacColl said in a friendly way. He smiled and stuck the bug repellent back into his pocket.

"I ain't afraid," Skeets said.

"Then why don't you come along?" Mr. MacColl said. "I bet you know the forest like the back of your hand."

Skeets fell silent. He stared at the ground. Maybe if he took the stranger a different way he could keep his pool a secret. "Okay, I'll go."

"Good," said Mr. MacColl. He looked at Skeets's tattered sneakers. "Go get your boots. I'll wait."

"I don't need boots," Skeets said. "I'm ready now."

Mr. MacColl looked up at the towering, thickly forested Catamount Ridge. For a second, Skeets thought he saw him shudder. "Very well, then," he said. "Lead the way."

The duo entered the woods behind the barn, with Skeets in front. It suddenly got dark. The sun was unable to penetrate the canopy of leaves. Mr. MacColl began to sweat. Skeets thought that odd because, in the shadows of the tall, thick trees, the air was cool.

The path split in two. To the left, it ran up a steep incline and disappeared behind several large moss-enshrouded boulders that had fallen from the ridge a million years ago. To the right, it meandered beside a small creek. Here the land was not so steep. Skeets took this path. Hunters like his father and uncle always went this way. It was much easier, drifting lazily along the contours of the ridge. The other path, just a slit in the woods like a narrow knife blade, went straight up. It took a hardy hiker to conquer it.

"Ah," sighed Mr. MacColl, "the path of least resistance. You seemed a little hesitant about which trail to take." He dabbed at his forehead with a handkerchief. He then looped it around his forehead and tied it. "Where do you suppose the other path goes?"

"Nowhere," Skeets said. "It's a dead end."

They hiked in silence. Behind him, Skeets heard Mr. MacColl's labored breathing. It didn't sound like someone out of breath. Rather, thought Skeets, it sounded like someone in a panic. The breaths came in short gasps. They reached a place where a tree had fallen across the creek. Skeets used it as a bridge, effortlessly bounding over the small stream. He turned and waited for Mr. MacColl to catch up.

The stranger halted by the fallen tree. His face was pale and dripped with sweat. Skeets sensed Mr. MacColl wasn't going to cross.

"Let's rest for a moment." Mr. MacColl was panting. "My leg's killing me."

He sat on the gnarled root of the tree. Looking up through the canopy of leaves, he pictured himself trapped among the branches, blood dripping down his mangled arm and leg. Below, he heard the faint voices of the Vietcong. "I'm not ready for this," he said. "We better head back."

Skeets bounded back across the fallen tree. "We can go slower, if you want." He leapt off the tree onto the creek's muddy banks. "I mean, I'm in no hurry. And the trail's pretty tame. Hunters use it all the time."

"Next time," Mr. MacColl said. "I've got to work up to it. Get the strength back in my bum leg."

Skeets knew it was none of his business, but he couldn't help asking, "Were you in a car accident, Mr. MacColl?"

"I was a navy pilot back in the sixties, flying a bombing mission over the jungles of Vietnam. My plane was shot down, crashed in the mountains."

A *bomber pilot!* Skeets remembered Mr. MacColl had mentioned that the first night they'd met. *Wow, a bomber pilot. Jungles, too!* Skeets didn't know what to say next. But he certainly wondered about the wound.

Mr. MacColl stood. "You don't mind if we head back now, do you?"

"Naw. I come up here all the time. I love the woods."

"It sure looks that way," Mr. MacColl said, "the way you ran across that old fallen-down tree like a tightrope artist."

They retraced their steps along the small creek and out of the forest. The sudden sunlight blinded them both for a moment. Mr. MacColl's face and posture relaxed. "It sure is dark in there," he said.

"In some places it's like night," Skeets said. "But once you get way up on top of Catamount Ridge, then it's as bright as it is here by the barn. There're not so many trees. And you can see for miles around. All the way into Canada. I love it up there!"

"I'd like to go up there with you sometime," Mr. MacColl said. "I'll keep working on my bum leg and when I feel it's strong enough, you can take me to the top."

"Sure," Skeets said. He figured when the time came he'd take Mr. MacColl up the old hunters' trail, far away from his secret pool. The view was just as pretty. And besides, it was an easier hike.

Mr. MacColl pulled off his handkerchief and dabbed at his sweaty forehead. The color in his cheeks started to return. His breathing eased. "I couldn't help but notice how agile you are," he said. "Quick across that log."

"Oh, I ain't so quick. I just know the woods, that's all."

"Maybe so, but I bet you'd make a good track athlete."

Skeets felt the blood rush to his face. He was no athlete. Anyone could see that. "I don't have time for track."

"Baloney! Why, I bet you'd make a good hurdler. Maybe even a good pole-vaulter. You ever think of going out for track?"

"I went out for the baseball team. Everybody made fun of me."

"Well, nobody would make fun of you in track—especially if you could run and jump as well as they could."

Skeets turned away from Mr. MacColl. "Dontcha see? I'm too small."

"Size has nothing to do with it. How many kids bigger than you can scoot across that log back there the way you do? Why, they'd be afraid they'd slip off and fall in the creek."

"But I don't give it no thought. It's just somethin' I do."

"That's right, Skeets. And it'd be the same with hurdling." Mr. MacColl rubbed his bad arm. Then he looked at Skeets. "Come up to your room, I want to show you something."

What could he have in my room that I don't know about?

When they got there, Mr. MacColl went over to his suitcase and rummaged around for a bit. He pulled out a frayed poster, unfolded it, and spread it on Skeets's bed.

"See, that poster there says 'No Excuses!' I keep it with me at all times. It reminds me to never feel sorry for myself." Skeets looked at the poster of a man jumping a hurdle as if he were in outer space. "Let me tell you a story about that guy. That's Glenn Davis, a friend of mine—a mentor, in fact. He was from the West Virginia coal mines and later from a small Ohio town. His mother and father both died on the same day when he was but fifteen, about your age. He was angry with his parents for leaving him an orphan. He'd pick fights with anybody, it didn't matter how big they were or how strong. And he was like you, small in stature.

25

He'd fight, get hauled into the principal's office, threatened with expulsion, but he'd give the excuse that it was because his mother and father had died on him and he couldn't help himself. He was headed for a dead end. What saved him was he got into sports and took his anger out on the football field and on the track. He went to Ohio State on a football scholarship. But when his coach, Woody Hayes, saw how fast he was, he turned him over to the track coach. At Ohio State he set several world records in the 440-yard dash and went on to win three gold medals in the Olympics, in 1956 and 1960, as an intermediate hurdler. He was one of the best there ever was. In his honor his hometown erected his statue in front of the library and produced this poster. And Glenn's motto? Right up there on the poster. *No Excuses!*"

Mr. MacColl took a deep breath. Then he said to Skeets, "Can you get me a yardstick?"

"Yardstick? Sure," he said, looking at the poster.

"Good. I'll meet you outside."

Skeets got a yardstick his mother kept in the broom closet while Mr. MacColl went out into the yard. Skeets came out of the house and handed it to Mr. MacColl, who held it against his leg and marked a spot just above that, measuring thirty-nine inches. Next, he held the yardstick out in front of him, vertically, and at the height he'd just measured.

"Now I want you to step back about ten yards," Mr. MacColl ordered, "and then run forward and hurdle the yardstick."

Skeets felt his blood race. He ran forward and vaulted the yardstick. It was like he was up on Catamount Ridge dashing over boulders and fallen logs. He cleared it with little effort.

"See, I told you," Mr. MacColl said. "Easy as pie."

"But that's only a yardstick," Skeets countered. "It's no hurdle."

Mr. MacColl nodded. "Now go in the barn and drag out those two sawhorses in the corner of the stall."

Skeets obeyed him. When he came out of the barn, he was shown where to place them, one after the other. The distance between them was about ten yards. Mr. MacColl stood ten yards behind the last hurdle, holding out the yardstick. Hollering to

Skeets, he ordered him to run and jump over the sawhorses and the yardstick.

Skeets crouched like a sprinter. He burst forward, clearing the sawhorses and the yardstick—easy as pie.

"You're a natural, like a small panther," Mr. MacColl said. "Size has nothing to do with athletic ability. I bet with a little training you could be a star on the track team."

"You're just sayin' that to make me feel good 'cause you're living in my room."

Even though this was easy, Skeets remembered his embarrassment when he'd tried out for the baseball team. He couldn't hit, and he couldn't field. He saw himself stumbling over hurdles as the track team stood by and laughed, Emile laughing the hardest. And if Becky was on the track as well, practicing, she'd be laughing, too. He'd bet on it. "I can never be a track star."

"You cleared three hurdles like they weren't even there," Mr. MacColl said. "You could do ten easy. By the end of the season, I bet you'd be a top hurdler on the team. And if you'd like, I'd help coach you. I ran track myself, a long time ago."

"You'd teach me?"

"I'd teach you to run hurdles. And to throw the shot put, the javelin, do the pole vault. If you wanted, you could compete in a decathlon. Why, I'd help you become a decathlete."

"A decathlete? What's that?" Skeets sat on top of a sawhorse.

"It's an athlete who does ten track events in a single meet," Mr. MacColl said. "Ten events to glory! 'Deca' is Greek for 'ten.' It takes two days to complete a decathlon. On the first day, you sprint one hundred meters, long-jump, toss the shot, high-jump, and run four hundred meters." Mr. MacColl grew animated. "On the second day, you start with the one-hundred-ten-meter high hurdles, then the discus, the pole vault, the javelin, and end up running the metric mile—fifteen hundred meters. You're dog-tired. You swear you'll never do another decathlon again as long as you live. Ah, but what a glorious two days. And then you can't wait for the next time."

"Do you have to win every event to be the champion?" Skeets asked.

"You sure don't. In fact, you don't even have to win a single event to be champ."

"How can that be?"

"The decathlon is scored on a point system. Depending on how well you do in each event, you get so many points. For example, you might get seven hundred points for running the hundred-meter dash in, say, eleven point seven seconds. Pick up six hundred points by long-jumping about twenty feet. You could be second or third in every event and score six thousand points, while another decathlete might win four or five events but do poorly the rest of the way, score a total of maybe fifty-eight hundred points, and at the end of the two-day competition come in second."

"Does that happen often?"

"All the time. The best example was in the 1960 Olympics. C. K. Yang, from Taiwan, won five of the ten events. He even beat Rafer Johnson, the American, in seven events. Yet Rafer won the gold medal because he'd stayed close to C. K. Yang in the events he lost and scored big in the events he won."

"Have there ever been small decathletes that were good?"

"Certainly," said Mr. MacColl, sounding pleased to be an amateur Olympic historian. "I knew one of the best, smallest decathletes there ever was. Jeff Bennett from Oklahoma. Jeff was only five feet eight inches tall and weighed a mere one hundred fifty pounds. He missed winning a medal in the 1972 Olympics in Munich, Germany, by ten points."

"Did you ever do a decathlon? It sounds like you did."

"Many times," Mr. MacColl's voice trailed off, turning so soft Skeets barely heard him. Then, louder, he asked, "Do you know what they call the Olympic decathlon champion?"

Skeets shook his head. He had no idea.

Thinking back to his glory days before the plane crash, Mr. MacColl, his voice cracking like something dry was caught in his throat, said, "The world's greatest athlete."

7

The horse stall was a fifteen-by-fifteen-foot windowless square. The floor was earthen. Above it was an empty hayloft. The loft stretched from one end of the barn to the other. Every August, Skeets and his father filled it with hay. Mr. Stearns worked like a horse to turn the stall into a livable room. When his evening chores were finished, Skeets helped out. And so did Mr. MacColl.

They put in a floor of rough-hewn planks and covered it with an old carpet they'd found in the attic. They insulated the walls. They put in a bay window, facing Catamount Ridge, and set up a closet with a curtain for a door. According to Mr. MacColl's wishes, they lined one wall with floor-to-ceiling bookcases. They built a crude table and erected a canvas cot. A woodstove was the last thing they put in.

According to Mr. MacColl's wishes, they did not wire the room for electricity.

"Don't you think this is weird?" Skeets said to his father after they'd finished. The sudden appearance of Mr. MacColl still troubled him. In fact, he'd slept little in the past two weeks. "No electricity. No TV. No phone. It's like he's running away from something."

Mr. Stearns shrugged. "Your uncle Jacques said something about him coming up here to the Northeast Kingdom to get his life back together. Something to do with him being a cripple and all."

"It's just annoying to have a guy like that around," Skeets said.

"I never ask a man about his life," Mr. Stearns said. He put down his hammer. His hands were gnarled from years of hard labor. Rough as they were, he used them to wipe sweat off his forehead. "And besides, he's paying us to build this room and paying us to rent it. The way farming is today, we can use the extra cash."

Between farm chores, school, and meals, it took them almost three weeks to remodel the stall into a livable room.

When Mr. MacColl finally moved out of Skeets's room and into his new place, he carried in a bundle of clothes from the back of his station wagon and hung them in the closet behind the curtain. He lugged in boxes of books and set them in the bookcases. He brought in a portable radio and placed it on a shelf next to the books. He tossed a sleeping bag onto the cot. Beneath the cot he shoved another pair of hiking boots. From his suitcase, he took out the bottle of whiskey and shot glass and stuck them under the cot, next to his hiking boots. Then, on a wall, he tacked up the large black-and-white poster of Glenn Davis—"No Excuses!"

That night, as Skeets hooked the cows to the milking machine, he saw light flicker from under the door. He moved among the cows in his squeaky rubber boots. Every time he clamped the suction cup over a cow's udder, he stood up and looked at the flickering light. Sometimes he had to stand on his tiptoes to see over the rump of a cow. Now and then he spotted under the door a shadow moving back and forth. Once again Mr. MacColl was pacing.

When curiosity finally got the better of him, Skeets took off his boots and climbed into the hayloft, strewn with hay. He knew it was wrong. He felt his heartbeat quicken. If he got caught there'd be no telling what the stranger might do.

The hayloft was mostly pitch-dark, except for a few rays of light streaming up between the cracks in the floorboards over the horse stall. Skeets crept toward the light. There was enough hay left over from last year to muffle any noise he made. Holding his breath, he peered through one of the cracks. Below him, Mr. MacColl paced back and forth. His clothes were the same as before. His hair was still in a ponytail. A sleeping bag was spread across the cot. On the crude table were a kerosene lamp and a portable radio. A book was open next to the lamp. Skeets's eyes moved to the bookcases he'd helped his father build. Half of the shelves were filled with books. He wondered why all the books, and what were they about.

Mr. MacColl stopped pacing. He hunched over an open book.

30

He kneaded the back of his neck with his good hand as he read something Skeets figured must be important. He began pacing again.

Looking directly down on Mr. MacColl, Skeets noticed he had a tiny bald spot. *The things you notice when you're tall,* he thought. *Or the things you missed because you were short.*

Mr. MacColl finally sagged down on the bunk bed like a tired old man. He pressed his good arm against his forehead as if he had a headache. He stayed that way for at least fifteen minutes. At first Skeets thought he'd fallen asleep. But then Mr. MacColl blinked and Skeets knew he was in deep thought.

After a bit, a pang of guilt swept over Skeets because he felt like a spy, a dirty, rotten sneak. Sneaking around and spying was wrong and he knew it. Feeling guilty, he backed away and climbed down. He got back into his rubber boots. Maybe Mr. MacColl wasn't a gangster after all, he thought. Gangsters didn't read.

Back in his own bed at last, Skeets fell asleep with the image of a forlorn Mr. MacColl in his kerosene-lit room, pondering an open book.

8

On a Monday afternoon, Skeets Stearns walked up to Coach Norton. He said, "I'd like to run the hurdles." He hadn't told Emile he was trying out for the track team. He didn't want to be laughed at twice in one day. He waited for Coach Norton's surprised gasp and then firm rejection. After all, last year Coach Norton had cut him from the baseball team.

"That's great, Skeets," he said instead. He wore glasses and a baseball cap with the letters HF stitched on the front. A stopwatch and brass whistle dangled from his neck. He was about sixty years old, with gray, balding hair and deep wrinkles around his eyes. "I noticed you in the bleachers a few weeks ago and hoped you'd come out for the team. I can always use help in the hurdles."

Coach Norton's friendly acceptance came as a surprise. "Well, I don't know if I can help, but I think I'd like to try," Skeets said.

"Let's see what you can do and we'll take it from there." Coach Norton tugged at the bill of his cap.

"Yes sir. Whatta I do?"

"Go on over to the track, where the hurdles are set up. I'll tell you to get set and then blow the whistle. You take off as fast as you can. Jump over all the hurdles and run through the finish line. I'll time you and we'll see."

Skeets trotted to the starting line. As he crouched, awaiting Coach's whistle, he felt every eye on him. Especially Emile's hard, dark eyes. Standing off to the side of the track, waiting for their turn to run the hurdles, were three girls, including Becky Winslow. He'd forgotten she'd be there practicing. There was a slight pain in his chest, near his heart. He knew it was from nervousness.

Coach Norton took the stopwatch from around his neck. "Get set!" he yelled.

Skeets tensed his muscles. He gulped in a big breath of air.

The moment Coach Norton blew into his whistle Skeets darted toward the first hurdle. He jumped it and headed for the next one. He reached it in four steps, and bounded over. After another four steps he found himself clearing the third hurdle. Then the fourth and fifth and sixth. It seemed easy, he thought. But he nicked the seventh with the calf of his leg. The eighth he banged with his foot and stumbled into the ninth, knocking it and himself over. He scrambled to his feet, a rip in his jeans and blood seeping from a small cut on his knee, and jumped the last hurdle. Staggering across the finish line, he wanted to find a place to hide.

Instead of throwing up his arms in despair, Coach Norton said, "Not bad, Skeets. Not bad at all." He checked his stopwatch. "With the fall, and wearing street clothes and all, you made it in eighteen point two seconds. With some training—and no falls—I bet you could run the hurdles in about sixteen seconds."

"Is that good?" Skeets asked. His knee hurt, but he refused to look at it.

"Sixteen seconds would get you into the county meet. I'd say that's helping my team, wouldn't you?"

"But I fell," Skeets said.

"For your first time you ran a respectable time—in spite of tripping." Coach Norton hung the stopwatch around his neck. "You four-stepped between each hurdle and for a lad your size that's good. You were thrown off stride when you nicked the seventh hurdle. With practice you won't fall."

"Whatta I do now?" Skeets felt the pride in his chest. He felt that way only up on Catamount Ridge. Had Becky watched him the whole time?

"Practice jumping over three hurdles. Keep it up until you feel comfortable. Try to maintain four steps between each hurdle. And if you can afford them, buy yourself a set of track shoes, with spikes. Tomorrow I'll get you a uniform."

"Right, Coach!" Before running back to the starting line, Skeets added, "And I wanna do the decathlon, too."

Coach Norton's mouth fell open. "The decathlon?"

"Yep," said Skeets.

"Well, I'll be."

Skeets sprinted to the starting line. He felt ten feet tall. He dashed over three hurdles. He did it again and again and again, thinking of the Glenn Davis poster. *No Excuses!*

Skeets didn't hear Emile McIntosh come up behind him.

"Whatta we got here, a new track star or what?"

Skeets jumped around. Emile stood with his hands on his hips.

"Hi, Emile."

"What's made a shrimp like you come out for track?"

"I guess Mr. MacColl. He said I'd make a good decathlete. That's an athlete who does ten events. The Olympic champion is called the world's greatest athlete."

Emile snorted. "You might be an okay hurdler. Well, maybe, but you'll never be a great athlete like me—not at this school." He sauntered away, heading toward the shot put ring. Skeets watched him. He wondered why Emile always ridiculed him. Maybe Emile was right. Maybe he'd never be a great athlete. That wasn't his plan, anyway. He'd only wanted to make the team—and now he had.

Turning back toward the track, Skeets looked at the long row of hurdles—ten in all, stretching 110 meters along the front of the bleachers. For a moment he saw himself atop Catamount Ridge, dashing close to the edge. One misstep and he'd plummet three thousand feet to his death, and he knew it. Compared to Catamount Ridge, the hurdles were nothing. Skeets crouched again, leapt forward, and tackled each hurdle. Instead of taking on three, as Coach Norton had suggested, he attacked all ten. He saw each one as a fallen log and in his mind's eye he was back on the ridge, running for all he was worth. He cleared all the hurdles. He stopped, panting. He looked back down the track, then toward the shot put ring. Emile, standing in the ring, glared back at him.

Becky was nowhere to be seen.

9

The only untilled level piece of land on the Stearns farm was between the barn and the cornfield. Here Mr. MacColl and Skeets built a jumping pit. They built a crude ring for tossing the shot and discus. They set up a row of five homemade hurdles, where Mr. MacColl taught Skeets the proper form. He also erected a place for the youngster to pole vault, using bales of hay to cushion the landing.

At first Skeets's parents were not keen on their son going out for the track team when there were farm chores to do.

"When are you going to have the time to learn all this running and jumping stuff?" his father had said. But his mother saw the look in Skeets's eyes and knew it was for the best. "Let him be," she said to her husband. "He's just a boy. Let him be."

Meanwhile, Coach Norton, to help Skeets train away from the high school, allowed him to borrow from the school a shot put, discus, javelin, and fiberglass vaulting pole. He didn't have time to instruct his newest decathlete in every event and still handle the baseball team that had potential to become county champions, and so he allowed him to take the equipment home.

"Who's this guy teaching you how to become a decathlete?" Coach Norton asked while handing Skeets a javelin.

"He's from New York City, and he's living in our barn. I don't understand why, Coach, 'cept maybe he's embarrassed because he's crippled and all. He has a bum arm and limps. But he knows all about hurdlin'. He told me he used to run track when he was younger. Before he got hurt in a plane crash when he was in the navy."

"Is that so? Well, you bring him to the first track meet of the season. I'd like to meet him."

Skeets nodded. He lugged the javelin, shot, discus, and vaulting pole home. He had to cram the shot and discus into his knapsack along with his books and other school stuff. Thus began his crash course on the fundamentals of track and field. And a crash course it was.

"You've got to learn to be explosive," Mr. MacColl told him right off. "Life on the farm's made you strong for your size—like a young bull. You're naturally explosive. That'll be the key to your success." He showed Skeets how to explode off the starting blocks, how to explode across the shot ring, and how to explode upward in the high jump. He taught him how to rock backward in the vault when the pole bent, to turn upside down and ride the pole as it catapulted him skyward.

"You're a natural, Skeets," he said. "I bet the days you spent prowling up on Catamount Ridge turned you into a natural athlete."

Skeets blushed, not just from Mr. MacColl's praise, but also every time he crash-landed when he tripped over a hurdle or a missed vault.

"Nobody taught you how to run and jump. Yet you do it as easily as anyone I've ever seen."

Skeets had to admit that he loved to run and jump. Up on the ridge that's all he did. He'd done it since he first went up there, and he couldn't remember how far back that was. Maybe when he was seven or eight? Maybe even younger. It seemed he'd always been darting over the rocky ledges and fallen trees, breathing in the mountain air, and loving every minute of it.

After a while, Emile McIntosh appeared at the farm. Word had gotten around the track team that there was a cripple living in the hayloft of the Stearns barn. Rumor said he'd killed a man in a gambling dispute and was hiding from the law. Either that, or his arm had been shot off during a daring bank holdup. Now he was a wanted man. Emile had spread most of the rumors; after all, he'd met the man and claimed he had cow dung for brains. The only truthful thing Emile said about the cripple was that he knew something about track. The way Skeets performed in the hurdles after a few weeks of training drew Emile back to the Stearnses' farm.

"I was wonderin'," he said, "if you'd show me a few tricks to make me put the shot a little better." He looked at Skeets. "You've been helpin' Skeets out, maybe you'd teach me a thing or two."

Mr. MacColl limped to the big stone by the barn. He sat down on it. He rubbed his bum leg with his good hand. He squinted at Emile, who was standing directly in the sunlight. "Why do you want to learn from me?"

"Coach don't know much about the shot. Baseball's his game. If I'm gonna be state champion I need to pick up a few pointers. Get an edge on the competition. A couple of weeks ago you told me something about speed. You said I needed more speed. I wanna know how to go about gettin' that speed."

"Your goal is to be state champ. That's it?" Mr. MacColl continued to rub his leg.

"That's it," said Emile.

"Why do you want to be state champ?"

"Who doesn't want to be state champ?"

"Tell me, Skeets," Mr. MacColl asked, "why have you taken up track? To be state champ?"

"I'll never be that good!" Skeets said.

"Then why?"

Skeets squeezed his hands into small fists. "I guess 'cause I love to run and jump. It makes me feel free. You know, like a bird, or something. Like a mountain lion." It upset him that he'd told on himself, spilling a secret he'd never meant Emile to know. Now he knew it. He'd now be tormented worse than ever.

"A mountain lion?" Emile said, practically sneering at Skeets. "That's silly. You compete to win, dontcha, MacColl?"

"Don't call me MacColl. It's disrespectful," Mr. MacColl said with a coolness that caught both Skeets and Emile off guard. "You call me Mr. MacColl or Bill." He stopped rubbing his lame leg. "Winning's important," he said, "but not everybody can win. And just because you don't win doesn't mean you're a loser. You do the best you can. That's all anybody can do because somebody always comes along who's bigger, stronger, and faster. So you do the best you can."

"Yeah, but I'm the strongest boy in the county! There ain't anybody bigger than me!"

"We call him the Big Apple," Skeets chimed in. "You know,

like New York City, because his name's McIntosh."

"All I need is to be faster," Emile said. "Like you told me, I gotta have speed! I wanna do better. I know I can do better, Mr. MacColl. I just don't know how."

"Okay, Emile. Pick up the old iron orb, and I'll try and show how you can be the best shot-putter you can be."

From then on Emile showed up when he could, to learn to be a better shot-putter. And for the moment his bullying died down.

10

"I can't believe our boy is on the track team!" Mrs. Stearns said. She was in the stands, sitting between her husband and Mr. MacColl. For a Vermont spring day, with the Green Mountains looming high over the village, it was comfortably warm—in the high forties, overcast, and windy. They were bundled against the wind, snug in sweaters and sharing a blanket draped over their legs. Below them, three high school teams loosened up for the start of a triangular meet. It was the first competition of the season. On all sides, hopes ran high.

Coach Norton believed he had his best team in years at Hackett's Falls. He was pleased with his newest member. Knowing Skeets had his eyes on the decathlon, he'd placed him in four events—the most allowed in a high school track meet. The 110-meter high hurdles, of course. But also the pole vault, javelin, and the mile. Emile was competing in the shot put, discus, and javelin. In the javelin they'd have to face off against each other, as well as against the other competitors.

"I never knew Skeets liked track," Mrs. Stearns said. "I always thought he'd rather spend his time roaming Catamount Ridge."

Mr. MacColl turned toward her. "I think his love of the woods has given him a love for track. Watch how he runs and jumps. He didn't learn that from any coach. He learned it by running free in the forest."

Hackett's Falls failed to place a runner in the first two events, the 3,000-meter run and the 100-meter dash. Meanwhile, with the pole vault and high jump already under way, the track was readied for the high hurdles. Skeets had yet to take a jump in the pole vault. His opening height was nine feet. The bar was at eight.

As the hurdlers were called to the starting line, his stomach was a tight knot. His legs shook. He wanted to throw up. He knew everyone in the race was a veteran hurdler, including his teammate Billy Abbott, who'd run a 15.7. All Skeets wanted was a time under seventeen seconds. He wanted to finish standing up, too, and not crash—certainly not in front of his parents, Mr. MacColl, and, sitting in the student section, Becky. Particularly Becky.

The hurdles looked higher than the standard thirty-nine inches. Crouching in the starting blocks, he wanted to look at Becky to see if she was watching. Instead, he looked toward his parents in the stands where his small fan club sat. Behind them Catamount Ridge rose up in its leafy green splendor.

He turned his attention to the starter's commands.

The gunshot startled Skeets. He hesitated in the blocks while the other hurdlers broke free. He was on the outside track—closest to the bleachers. By the time he got going, he was a full step behind the rest of the field. He cleared the first hurdle, still a step behind. As he ran he felt his heart pounding like a gong in his chest.

Abbott was already ahead of everyone. He took the hurdles effortlessly. Unless he suffered a misstep, he'd win.

Skeets closed on two runners, catching them by the time he reached the sixth hurdle. He was surprised when he passed them. The exhilaration that swept through him at that moment was wonderful. He wasn't the worst hurdler ever! And then, as he charged across the finish line, he looked quickly to his right. He had nosed out another hurdler for third place.

Holding his hands against his head in utter joy, Skeets glanced up into the bleachers at his parents and Mr. MacColl and, this time, at Becky. They were all standing, cheering.

But he didn't have time to enjoy himself.

From the pole vault pit he heard his name being called by the official there. "Stearns on deck!"

"Uh-oh!" he thought. "I'm next!"

As soon as one of the timers gave him permission to leave, Skeets bolted to the pole vault pit—without learning his hurdle time. "You're up," the vaulting official said. "The bar's at nine feet."

Breathing heavily, Skeets grabbed his pole, a thirteen-foot

fiberglass Catapult. He trotted to the top of the runway. In practice he'd cleared ten feet. But now, under game conditions, the crossbar appeared, like the hurdles, higher than anything he'd tried before.

"Calm down," he told himself.

He held the pole upright in both hands. It looked like a knight's lance. And then, like a knight on a fast steed, Skeets headed down the runway. He slammed the pole into the planting box. The sudden jolt rocked him backward. Instantly, he lifted off—kicking his legs upward, trying to turn his entire body upside down. The pole bent. For a fraction of a second Skeets hung upside down without moving. The pole straightened out. And as it did, Skeets was flung over the crossbar. He twisted his body so he faced the ground. The crossbar was directly below him. He crashed into it as he fell back to earth. He and the crossbar thudded against the mats at the same time. It was a miss.

Skeets jumped off the mats. "I was over the crossbar," he scolded himself.

"Way over."

Hackett's Falls' leading vaulter, Tommy Patneau, came over to Skeets. Patneau never entered the vault until the crossbar reached twelve feet. His best jump was thirteen-eight, the school record. "You had it," he said, putting his arm around Skeets's shoulders. "Your step was off about a foot. That means you went straight up and straight down, leaving no room to miss the crossbar. I bet if you lengthen your run by a foot you'll clear your next jump."

"You really think so?" Skeets asked, surprised that Tommy would help him.

"Yeah, I think so."

By moving his run back a foot, Skeets easily cleared the crossbar on his next jump. As he rolled off the mats, he realized he hadn't thanked Tommy for the tip. But he didn't have time to look for him. The javelin was starting on a field behind the bleachers, in a safe place away from athletes and spectators.

"I've got to throw the javelin," Skeets said to the vaulting official. "I'll be back as soon as I can."

The official didn't care about Skeets. "You better be back soon because in about ten minutes I'm moving the bar up to nine feet six inches and if you're not ready to go I'll declare it a missed jump."

Skeets hurried off the field, across the track, and past the bleachers to the other field where the javelin was held. He reported to the official there, a white-haired, heavyset coach from one of the rival schools, named Bob Tipson, who'd almost made the U.S. Olympic team in 1968. Tipson was patient with the young athletes. He knew they were just learning, and it was important to him that they got their throws in without any added pressure. There were eight competitors—mostly big boys with bulging biceps. The biggest and most muscular, of course, was Emile.

"I can't believe you're throwin' the jav," Emile said, as Skeets came running up to him. In Emile's hands the javelin looked like a toothpick. "I wonder what Coach was thinkin' when he put you in this event."

"Coach says size has nuthin' to do with how far you can throw the javelin," Skeets said. "So does Mr. MacColl. He said it's all in the technique."

"Maybe so. But you watch me and you'll soon find out size has everything to do with it."

Because he'd gotten to the javelin as it was starting, Skeets wasn't given a warm-up toss. He was assigned to throw last.

Emile was first. He hefted the javelin in his powerful right hand. He jogged down the runway, gaining momentum the closer he got to the release line. He then dropped the javelin to his side, straightened his arm so it extended behind him, and started to scissors-step. Ten feet from the release line he began his throw, roaring like a bull elephant. His arm came forward with slingshot speed. The javelin sailed high and deep, and thudded into the distant turf. Emile's toss measured 169 feet.

He came up to Skeets. "Like I told ya, size has everything to do with it."

The next six throwers failed to match Emile's effort. The closest competitor, a lanky boy named Craig from Lyndonville, reached 163 feet.

"Stearns up!" hollered Coach Tipson. "McIntosh on deck! Craig in the hole!"

The javelin felt light in Skeets's hand, not nearly as heavy as the sapling he carried with him in the forest atop Catamount Ridge. He tried not to look at Emile. Emile stood along the sideline, watching him. Then Skeets took off, slowly at first, but going faster and faster. He held the javelin by his side. He quickly drew it behind him. Twisting off his front hip, he snapped his arm forward—leading with the elbow, the way Mr. MacColl had taught him. He felt the force of his throw from his chest along his shoulder and forearm to the tips of his fingers. The javelin jumped out of his hand with sudden violence. His foot snapped down within an inch of the release line. He turned quickly so he wouldn't fall over the line, committing a foul. The height of his throw surprised Skeets. The javelin stayed in the air like a bird caught on an updraft of wind. It rose higher and higher and then arched back to earth. When the javelin struck the ground, Skeets knew he'd done something remarkable. His heart pounding, he walked over to the official and bent down with him as he measured his throw.

"One hundred and seventy-seven feet five inches!"

Skeets didn't believe Coach Tipson. "One hundred seventy-seven feet five inches?" he asked incredulously.

"That's right, son. Nice throw!" Coach Tipson said. "McIntosh up! Craig on deck! Jackson in the hole!"

"But I'm not that strong to throw the javelin that far!"

"Son, I've seen a lot of high school javelin throwers over the years and you've got one of the best releases I've seen. When did Coach Norton become an expert in the javelin?"

"I dunno," Skeets said. "I was taught by Mr. MacColl."

"MacColl?" The name impressed Coach Tipson. "Not Billy MacColl, is it?"

"His first name is William," Skeets said. "He lives at our place."

Emile came down the runway. He roared his usual bull elephant roar as the javelin sprung from his hand.

"William MacColl." Coach Tipson watched Emile's javelin sail off. "Is he here?"

"Yes sir. He's up in the bleachers with my folks."

"Is he crippled? Walks with a limp and has no use of one of his arms?"

43

"He is crippled."

"Well, I'll be. Tell him Bob Tipson's here and wants to see him."

"Yes sir!"

Emile's second effort was shorter than his first by three feet. He slammed his right fist into his left hand in disgust. He did not look toward Skeets.

Skeets realized he had to be back at the pole vault pit. "I'll be right back, Coach Tipson," he said, scooting back toward the bleachers. He raced in front of the stands, waving up at his fan club. Mr. MacColl flashed him a thumbs-up sign. Skeets stopped for a moment and yelled up to him, "Coach Bob Tipson, the guy who's officiating the javelin, wants to see you after the meet!"

"Hurry up," snapped the pole vault official. "Another second and I'll declare you absent and mark you down for a miss."

Skeets scooped up his pole and hurried to the top of the runway. He checked his marker. "Let's go, Skeets! This height is a piece of cake for you." It was Tommy Patneau shouting words of encouragement. Tommy hadn't yet jumped. Skeets held the pole in front of him, steadied himself as best he could, focused on the crossbar, and headed down the runway. Shoving the pole into the planting box, he rose upward. He sailed over the crossbar, this time clearing it with ease. He tumbled onto the mats. "All right, Skeets!" yelled Tommy.

But there was no time to rest. Hopping off the mat, Skeets headed back to the javelin. His final two throws never matched his first. But that effort gave him first place. It was a stunning win, and for the rest of the meet Emile avoided Skeets. But he watched him wherever he went—from the pole vault to the javelin, back to the pole vault, and then, finally, the mile.

In the vault, Skeets cleared eleven feet, placing third. Tommy Patneau won with a thirteen-foot jump. For Skeets, a first and two thirds—and he was not yet finished.

Lining up with eleven other runners for the start of the mile, he'd no inkling of his grand performance. His only thought was to be ready for the crack of the starter's pistol. The moment he heard the pistol's sharp report, he broke ahead of the pack. He moved effortlessly over the track. Running on flat, open land was much easier than the steep ravines and gullies and the narrow, wooded paths strewn with fallen timber and jagged boulders he encountered on Catamount Ridge. In his mind's eye he once again saw himself as the legendary mountain lion, loping through the forest. The image thrilled him. No one was going to catch him. He opened up a ten-yard lead. He stretched it to fifteen yards and then twenty. Once he dared to look over his shoulder. There wasn't a runner close enough to challenge him. He passed in front of the bleachers. He spotted his parents, but not Mr. MacColl. He looked for Becky and when he saw her he thought she flashed a smile his way. Crossing the finish line, he had a time of four minutes thirty-eight seconds. Skeets felt his life had changed forever.

Sweat glistened on his body as his teammates swarmed over him—not like when he'd failed to make the baseball team. They tousled his hair, pounded him playfully on the arm. Everyone but Emile, who stood silently beneath the bleachers. He'd won the shot put and discus and placed second in the javelin. He scored fifteen of Hackett's Falls' eighty-two points. Yet no one came to mob him.

After the team's congratulations, Skeets looked for his parents and Mr. MacColl. His parents were still in the stands. He ran up to them and hugged them.

"I'm proud of you, Skeets." Mrs. Stearns smiled. "You ran so beautifully, like a graceful animal."

"Gee, Mom, I—I—I dunno. I just love to run and jump. I dunno." Skeets looked around. "Where's Mr. MacColl?"

"He left," Mr. Stearns said.

"But why? When?"

"I don't know, son. He left soon after you told him that one of the officials wanted to see him."

"Coach Tipson?"

Mr. Stearns put his arm around Skeets's shoulder. "We better get home," he said. "We got plenty of chores to do before supper!"

When the Stearns family came down out of the bleachers, Skeets saw Becky off to the right. She smiled at him, a warm, inviting smile, a smile he'd never seen from her, and then quickly

45

turned away. As he watched her walk away, a strange sensation he'd never felt before swept through his entire body. Still watching Becky, he missed the last step and fell on his face.

11

That night the buzz around the dining room table was Skeets's debut performance in track and field. But the animated conversation was between Skeets and his parents. Mr. MacColl had chosen to stay in his room.

"Why isn't Mr. MacColl eatin' with us tonight?" Skeets asked with disappointment. "He's eaten with us every night since he's been here."

"Something's apparently bothering him," Mrs. Stearns said, passing a basket of rolls to Skeets. "He told us he wasn't feeling well, and asked if he could be excused from dinner."

Skeets grabbed a roll. It was warm in his hands. He broke it open and crammed a chunk into his mouth. "Did he say anything about me? I mean about my track stuff?"

"Don't talk with your mouth full," Mrs. Stearns said.

Skeets swallowed the chunk of roll. He washed it down with a gulp of milk. "Sorry, Mom. But did he say anything?"

"Only that you still had more to learn."

"You mean after what I did today I still gotta learn more?" Skeets crammed another piece of roll into his mouth.

"We can always learn more no matter how much we know," Mr. Stearns said. "It's a lot like farming. When you think you know everything something new always comes along and you got to learn all over again. Like new machinery. Or the latest fertilizer. Or some miracle seed that'll make your crops sprout quicker than jack flash."

"But I won two events."

"Beware of early success," warned his father.

Skeets knew he'd been boastful, and his family didn't like boastfulness in a person. "May I be excused?"

Mrs. Stearns saw that he'd cleaned his plate. "Finish your milk first."

Skeets downed the last remaining drops. He went outside.

Night had fallen. If Mr. MacColl didn't care how he did in track then maybe Becky didn't either. After all, she was the star runner on the girls' team. He remembered how she'd smiled at him. He visualized her face—the red hair, dark eyes, her tiny freckles, that smile, and then her lips. Did he have the guts to go to her track meet and let her see him watching her?

He sighed.

In the dark he couldn't see Catamount Ridge, but felt its power closing over him. He shuddered as if a chill wind, ignoring the warm spring evening, had swept down from its rocky heights. The barn was wrapped in darkness. There was no light from inside. What was troubling Mr. MacColl, he wondered.

Skeets turned and went back inside the comfort of his home.

As usual, Skeets was up early the next day, turning the cows loose. The cows took their time leaving the barn, their tails swishing back and forth. They took their old, worn, muddy path to the same old meadow. When the last cow trudged from the barn, Skeets grabbed a slop bucket and shovel and started cleaning out their nightly mess. His rubber boots squeaked as he walked. He emptied the bucket on a manure pile behind the barn. As he reentered the barn, he saw Mr. MacColl swaying unsteadily in the shadows. His hair was uncombed. He'd not bothered to pull it back in a ponytail. Instead, it fell across his shoulders like some dirty, stringy mop.

"You about done with your chores?" Mr. MacColl said.

"Yes sir. All I gotta do is finish haulin' away this manure and dump it onto the pile out back of the barn."

"Well, how'd you like to take me up on Catamount Ridge this morning?"

"I'd be happy to," Skeets said.

"I'll get myself ready, then. You knock on my door when you're ready."

"Yes sir."

His limp more noticeable than ever, Mr. MacColl went into his room and closed the door. Skeets filled another bucket. Wheeling around, he nearly bumped into Emile McIntosh.

"Jeezum crow! You startled me, Emile."

"Whatcha doin'?" Emile's huge frame blocked most of the sunlight streaming into the barn.

"Muckin' out the barn. Whatcha doin'?"

"Nuthin'," Emile said. "Look, I came over to congratulate you on yesterday's meet. I never thought you'd beat me in the jav, what with you bein' so shrimpy and all." Emile stuck out his hand. "Congrats!"

"Thanks," Skeets said, shaking Emile's big mitt. It wasn't like him to be tossing around congratulations so easily. He waited for Emile to say something unkind, like always.

Emile grabbed Skeets in a headlock and put his knuckles against Skeets's scalp. He rubbed down hard as Skeets squirmed to get loose. Emile laughed and let him go. "Just didn't want your performance to go to your head," he said. "Well, I'll be goin' now." He looked toward Mr. MacColl's room. "Maybe we can get together soon? I'd like to practice some more."

"Sure," Skeets said, his scalp still on fire.

"By the way," Emile said, "Becky told me to tell you hi. Wants to know if you'll be going to her track meet on Monday." He walked off, heading down the long gravel driveway to the road. With each step he kicked up little clouds of dust.

Skeets emptied the last bucket, thinking only of Becky. *She wants to say hi,* he thought. Again, he visualized her whole face. If only he had the nerve to ask her out, or something.

He took off his boots and put on his sneakers. Mr. MacColl came out of the barn wearing his hiking boots. His hair was yanked in a tight ponytail. As they took off across the back lot behind the barn, Skeets saw that his limp was worse. Or else he was dizzy. He seemed to reel more than limp.

"I meant to tell you that you looked pretty good yesterday," Mr. MacColl said. He was already sweating. His voice was distant, strange. "Especially in the javelin and the mile. But I saw areas where you can improve—and do even better."

"Emile was just here," Skeets said. "He wants to practice some more."

"Don't doubt it. He hasn't been listening to me—doing the

49

things I've been teaching him. But when you beat him in the jav he didn't like it one bit. Bet he doesn't want that to happen again."

"He's really not a javelin thrower," Skeets said. "He's best at the shot put."

"That's right. And he's afraid you might beat him in that event, too."

"Me?"

"Why not?"

"But that doesn't make any sense."

"Why? Because you're small?"

Skeets felt the blood rise to his face.

"You're strong and quick. You could do it."

"But I don't wanna beat Emile. He's my friend."

"Friend?" Mr. MacColl said.

"Yes," Skeets said.

Mr. MacColl rubbed his chin. "I saw you eyeing a red-haired lass at the track meet. She your girlfriend?"

Skeets's stomach tightened. How did he notice that? "Oh, that's only Becky Winslow."

"Only?"

Skeets didn't answer, stomach still in knots.

"Ever date her?"

"No," he said.

"Why not?"

Skeets didn't like the questions. "Let's head up the mountain, all right?"

They entered the woods. Darkness enveloped them. Where the path split, Skeets hesitated. If he went to the left he'd be taking Mr. MacColl toward his secret pool. When they first came into the woods, he'd been angry with him for taking over his room. He hadn't wanted to show him the part of Catamount Ridge he loved best because he figured he'd want to take that over as well. But everything had changed. Now he felt they were friends, although Mr. MacColl was acting strange. He'd taught him to be a track-and-field athlete. Skeets could repay that kindness by leading him up the hardest trail on the mountain to the pool.

"You wanna take the other trail today?" he asked. "The steep one?"

Looking at Mr. MacColl, Skeets saw he was breathing hard, as if he'd just run a mile. Beads of sweat formed a watery crown across his forehead. "Is your bum leg still not ready?"

Mr. MacColl found a rock and sat down. "Yeah," he said. He peered into the forest, to where sunlight failed to penetrate the trees.

He heard the Vietcong below, searching the underbrush. He heard their muffled voices. The clink of their canteens. The creak of their rifles, slung over their shoulders. He saw the conical hat of the Vietcong beneath him, spotted with his blood. He knew they'd kill him on sight. The dark forest was all around him. There was no way out.

Mr. MacColl slipped a tiny flask from inside his shirt. He uncapped it and took a swig. Only then did he look at Skeets. He wiped his mouth and stuck the flask back inside his shirt.

"I don't think we oughta take the steep trail today," Skeets said. "There's nuthin' up there anyway." Not knowing exactly what else to do, he headed off to the right, onto the old hunter's trail, gentle and easy to hike, and far away from his secret pool.

"Come back here!" Mr. MacColl said. Skeets looked back at him. He still sat on the rock, a sudden stranger. With his good arm, he beckoned Skeets to come forward. Skeets obliged. Mr. MacColl held out his hand. "Here, give me a pull up."

"Yes sir." Skeets took his hand. Mr. MacColl rose off the rock, swayed a moment. Skeets steadied him. "Why are you afraid of the woods?" Skeets didn't mean to ask that. "We better go back."

"You know what it's like to be scared?" There was anger in Mr. MacColl's voice, and it stabbed at Skeets.

Skeets nodded.

"I don't think you do." Mr. MacColl started back down the trail. Skeets watched him as he vanished into the shadows. Then Skeets, feeling an emptiness growing in his heart, turned to the left and, alone, took the steep trail that led up to his secret pool.

12

By the time Skeets reached the top of Catamount Ridge, thick clouds had settled in. He'd never been on the mountain when clouds rolled through, making it so foggy and damp it was hard to see. He felt chilled. The gnarled, scraggy pine trees looked eerie in the gloom. Storms were frequent in the North Country. The old saying was: "If you don't like Vermont weather, wait five minutes and it'll change." His father always quoted that line. Skeets made sure the days were sunny when he climbed the mountain. Whenever he felt a change in the air he turned back. But this time he was upset because Mr. MacColl had acted ornery and had been too darn nosy—asking if Becky Winslow was his girlfriend.

The weather was changing, getting worse. The cloud cover thickened. It was harder to see. More and more the darkness closed around Skeets. The wind picked up. The trees were ghostly shapes, bending in the wind.

He knew he had to get off the mountain right away.

Although he knew the way down as well as he knew the back of his hand, finding it was another matter.

Peering through the strange mist, Skeets thought the ground looked different. The familiar landmarks were lost. But he knew if he followed the downward slope of the mountain he'd be all right.

Before descending, he looked up at the dark sky. A great cloud swirled around him, cold on his face. He barely made out the tops of the trees. For a moment he thought he saw the dark shape of a huge bird roosting atop one of the ghostly pines. Instantly, as if on command, there was an opening in the cloud—a small slit—and sunlight broke through like a laser beam. It lit up the top of the tree. In the glow he saw a golden eagle. It looked at him with eyes like flashing steel. Then it turned quickly, as if sensing the approaching danger from another direction. With its great wings opening up, the golden eagle lifted off from the top of the tree and vanished into the cloud. And just as quickly, the slit closed and it was again dark.

Skeets had seen strange things on Catamount Ridge, but he'd never seen a golden eagle. He knew something had drawn its attention away from him, had shaken it off its roost. Maybe it was a bear. Bears didn't scare Skeets. They were too shy to be a bother. They always ran when they saw him. Whatever it was, Skeets had to be careful. He was certain eagles didn't flee so quickly unless they were scared off. He stood stock-still, straining to hear any kind of noise that might tell him something, give a clue as to what was hidden in the thick mist.

The shadowy forest gave up no sound.

Skeets cautiously moved down the ridge, aware that somewhere nearby in the gloom was the steep cliff, Catamount Ridge's defining landmark.

Mr. MacColl sat on his cot holding his head. On the floor between his feet was the flask, now drained empty. His head spun. His eyes hurt. His teeth ached. Why had he been so mean to the Stearns boy? He kicked at the flask, and missed. Outside he could hear the rain beginning. It was just a pitter-patter at first. Then it poured. A hard downfall, thundering against the rooftop with the sharp, steady rattle of a machine gun. It felt like a monsoon he'd once seen sweep through a village of thatched huts in Vietnam with flood force, swamping everything in sight—washing away most of the village. He staggered to the window. He could hardly see the Stearns farmhouse or the cornfield or the mountain. He remembered that somewhere up on the mountain Skeets was wandering around.

Even though Skeets had told him that he felt at home on the mountain, he wished he hadn't left him there alone. He cursed his drinking. He cursed his fear of the forest. He cursed that he was a cripple.

The rain rapped against the window glass, as if mocking him.

For a long time, he stared out the window. He watched the world fill up with a grayness, wet and miserable and depressing. He watched the spot at the edge of the woods where the path entered.

He watched and waited for Skeets to reappear, to come down off the mountain. He wanted to tell him he was sorry, that there were no excuses for the lousy way he'd acted. No excuses at all.

With each step, Skeets felt certain he was being followed. He'd once been followed by a mangy old dog that had gotten lost years ago and lived in the forest, wild as any mountain critter. The dog was shy, but probably remembered the time when it was owned by humans and got a square meal every day. Skeets caught a glimpse of it every so often, but the dog stayed well out of range. When he'd walked out of the woods into the clearing around the farmhouse, the dog barked at him. It refused to come out of the woods. Skeets never saw it again. At first, Skeets thought the old dog was trailing him, but then realized it was too quiet for a dog. Dogs didn't have retractable claws, like cats. When dogs ran, their claws clicked on the stones.

It was hard enough to stay on the path because of the darkness from the cloud. Whatever was out there made it difficult to concentrate on where he was going. He trusted his instincts. As long as he headed down he knew he'd be all right. He just couldn't stray too close to the cliff that he knew was somewhere off to his right. As he hiked, Skeets wondered how much of the mountain was shrouded by the cloud. He'd sometimes seen clouds cover half the mountain. Huge patches of fog had settled in the valley, but were usually gone by midmorning. This cloud was the thickest he'd ever seen. He was angry with himself for not seeing it roll in. One moment it was sunny, the next it was dark and damp. Now it was raining. Water ran into his eyes, making it even more difficult to see his way. He swiped at his eyes with his sleeve. But his sleeve was wet and it only made seeing worse. He blinked. Water fell from his eyes like tears.

Still, in the woods off to his left, Skeets sensed something there—watching him. Once he stood motionless for a long time. Rain dripped off his ears as he tried to listen as hard as he could. When at last he gave up straining to hear what he couldn't hear, he quickly turned and resumed his downhill march.

He took three steps and stumbled over the edge of the cliff.

Picking up his empty flask, Mr. MacColl gave it a shake to see if there was any whiskey in it. He then decided to go up Catamount Ridge to look for Skeets. First, he wanted one more drink. Reaching under his cot, he pulled out his stash of whiskey. He uncapped a bottle and tried to pour part of its fluid contents into the flask that he'd wedged between his knees. Most of the whiskey went on the floor. In his present state his shaky aim was poor. He tossed the flask onto the cot. Holding the now-half-empty whiskey bottle in his good hand, he stumbled out of his room and into the hard rain.

As he lurched across the backyard toward the woods, he took a swig from the bottle. Whiskey slopped against his chin. It mixed with the rain, rolling down the front of his neck.

Mr. MacColl took the path Skeets had always led him up. He stayed on it until he reached the place where it divided. He knew to the right was the easy route, the old hunter's trail. To the left was the steep route that only Skeets seemed to know, and was reluctant to share with him. Mr. MacColl was certain Skeets had taken that path. Steadying himself with more drink, trying to calm the terror that was building up first inside his mind, then inside his heart, he at last started up the mountain.

The trail was just a narrow swath through the underbrush. He'd never have known it was there if Skeets hadn't shown it to him. It started level, but soon curved up at a forty-five-degree angle. Immediately, the hiking got treacherous, especially for a gimpy man hindered by booze. The rain made the ground slippery as ice. After sliding backward several times, Mr. MacColl knew he couldn't climb the trail and hold onto the bottle at the same time. Taking a last swig, he set the bottle down. Then, using his good hand, he grasped branches from the bushes that hung over the trail and brushed against his face, and pulled himself up the steep, slippery incline.

Skeets thought his life was over.

When he had unwittingly pitched himself over the edge of the cliff, he fell through the cloud. But the drop was only ten or twelve feet. He thudded onto a ledge, turning his ankle. The pain shot up through his leg like a knife cut. He grabbed at his ankle with his hands. The pain eased a bit.

The ledge was narrow. Skeets knew immediately that he was lucky to have fallen where he'd fallen. A few feet either way and he'd have missed the ledge. With one hand, he reached out in the cloudy darkness, feeling for the edge. He didn't have far to reach. Just a couple of inches. There wasn't much room for him to move. Skeets felt his heart beating like it was located in his throat, not his chest. His throat felt tight. It was hard to swallow. He'd no idea what to do.

Mr. MacColl made it up the first steep incline. He concentrated so hard on making it that he'd no time to worry about his claustrophobic nightmare—the jungle so thick and dark. Along with the rain, sweat poured off his face.

The small trail veered off to the left again, this time rising ever so slightly. Huge boulders lined both sides. Breathing heavily, Mr. MacColl passed through this wall of rock that towered over him. On the other side, the trail turned upward. It was much steeper than the first incline. Rainwater splashed down the trail like a small cataract. Although it was steeper, the incline was not as difficult. The way it cut into the side of the mountain formed a flight of natural stairs. He mounted the stairs, limping more noticeably. His leg ached worse than it had in years. He wished he hadn't left the whiskey bottle. He longed for a drink.

The natural stairs switched back and forth. Scrubby pine grew on both sides. He was now hidden in tall trees like those in the jungle. He looked through the gray rain and saw far below him the vague outline of the Stearnses' farm. He was surprised at how high he'd already climbed.

His breathing was labored—not from fear so much as from physical exertion. The climb sobered him up.

The switchback trail continued on, inching upward. But just when he got comfortable with its openness, it angled into the mountain—changing into a ravine of fallen timber. He hiked the ravine, dodging the timber that was scattered like big matchsticks every which way.

Still, the trail was visible.

Mr. MacColl figured he was about halfway up Catamount Ridge. If it was like this the rest of the way then he was certain he'd make it to the top. The only thing worrying him was his leg. The pain was almost unbearable. He prayed it would hold out.

On he went.

After a bit he came to a stream. It ran down through the forest that grew thick on both sides. More startling than the thickness of the woods was that, when the trail reached the stream, it apparently ended. He felt the old terror taking hold once again. His mind thought crazy thoughts and started yelling at him. *Go back! Go back!*

Almost as quickly as the storm moved in, it moved away. For a split second, the sudden sunlight blinded Skeets. As his eyes adjusted to the light, the rays from the sun burned off the heavy mist. Still, steam rose from the rocky ledge as if from a damp fire.

It didn't take long for Skeets to realize the predicament he was in. His ankle hurt something awful. He didn't know if it was swollen, but he thought it was. He was afraid he wouldn't be able to stand. Even if he could he wondered if he could climb off the ledge. He pushed himself into a sitting position. His back rested against the side of the cold, wet cliff.

As the wind pushed the miserable cloud away, the valley opened up below him. Shielding his eyes from the brilliant sunlight, he looked toward the top of the cliff where he'd lost his way and fallen. The rocks were slick with rainwater. Spirals of steam curled upward as the sun began to dry the rocks.

As he tried to figure a way out of this dilemma before he panicked, Skeets heard a faint noise, the padding sound of a stalking animal coming closer to the edge of the cliff.

He plainly heard the animal sniffing the ground, its nose picking up his human scent. Through the spirals of steam, Skeets was sure he saw the animal the moment it peered over the edge of the cliff. Tawny in color, sharply pointed ears, fangs, and long whiskers. And then it pulled back and was gone, loping softly away.

Had he just seen the catamount?

Walking along the banks of the stream, Mr. MacColl found no trace of the trail. He limped across to the other side, soaking his boots in the effort. Again, he searched vainly for the trail. Like Skeets, it had vanished.

He sat down on a boulder in the middle of the stream. Although it was narrow, the stream showed the strength of the mountain whence it came. Its water was deep and ran rapidly over its rocky bed. For eons it had pulled boulders down off the top of the mountain, strewing them about as if they had weighed nothing. Many of the boulders dwarfed Mr. MacColl. Others were half his size. Where the boulders squatted in the water, pools formed behind them. As he stared at the boulders, almost mesmerized by the way they looked—like a parade of gray hippos marching down the mountain—it dawned on him that they were the stepping-stones to the summit.

Mr. MacColl knew there was no way he could jump from boulder to boulder, as he was certain Skeets had done. He marveled at the youth's athleticism and strength that allowed him to scamper up the mountain, using boulders as if they were rungs on a ladder. He just didn't have the strength in his leg to even dare to try. The best he could do was to wade through the stream. And he wondered if he even had the strength to do that.

Slipping off the boulder, he sank into the cold stream. The water reached his waist. The current was strong and nearly dragged him down. He fought against it. Once his footing felt secure on the pebbly bed of the stream, he pushed forward. The buoyancy of his body in the water took pressure off his bum leg. It was like he now had two strong legs. That fact gave him courage and elated him. He found himself smiling as he forced his crippled old self upstream.

Skeets dug his fingers into the side of the cliff. With great effort he hauled himself to his feet. He stood on one foot. The pain in his ankle had dulled. He put pressure on it. The ankle held. The injury wasn't as serious as he'd thought. But the moment he tried to lift himself up, the ankle buckled. He fell back.

As he sat back down on the ledge, the valley now clearly visible far below him, he knew he'd have to wait for someone to rescue him. First they'd have to know he was missing and then where he might be. And the only person who had those answers was probably too scared to do anything.

The worst thing Skeets could do was to let panic take over. Sitting there, trying hard to keep calm, he once again heard the faint noise of an animal. Again, it moved closer to the edge of the cliff.

Skeets twisted his head, looking up to the ledge where he'd fallen off.

Whatever was up there, it was coming after him. He felt his heart leap into his throat.

At times, Mr. MacColl had to swim. The stream was too deep to wade. His clothes dragged him down. He pushed off from the bottom with both legs, something he hadn't done in twenty years. Surfacing, he gulped in the fresh mountain air. Although he was afraid for Skeets, he was no longer afraid for himself. He felt exhilarated by his physical effort.

Eventually the stream got too steep to swim in. The water was a torrent rushing headlong down the mountain.

Dragging himself out of the stream, he fell on the bank. He was exhausted. He lay still for a while, collecting his strength and his thoughts, and waiting to dry out. He was now almost to the summit. The last two hundred yards he knew would be the toughest. There was no trail, at least none that he could see. He'd have to pick his way. There was a chance he'd get lost.

He stood and looked for a long time at the valley. The village of Hackett's Falls was so peaceful in its distance. He felt young again, and strong. He shrugged off the great sadness that wanted to engulf his whole being. And, turning, he began the last ascent of Catamount Ridge.

Nearer came the noise of the creature that was closing in on Skeets. Holding his breath, he waited for it to spring on him.

There was a click of feet on stone. A few pebbles dribbled over the side of the cliff, showering down on Skeets. He pawed at his eyes, rubbing away the pebbles. He squinted upward, expecting to see the legendary catamount.

He saw a shadow first. Then a face.

Peering down at him, with a smile as big as all outdoors, was Mr. MacColl.

13

"Skeets, grab my hand and I'll pull you up," Mr. MacColl said, as he reached down with his strong arm.

Skeets took his hand and was easily pulled off the ledge.

Looking at his rescuer, he was surprised to see he was soaked to the bone. His clothes were dark with water and clung to his body like another layer of skin. His breathing came hard.

"You made it up the river, didn't you?" Skeets was so surprised to see Mr. MacColl that for a moment he forgot about his dangerous predicament and his hurt ankle. Mr. MacColl nodded, still gasping for breath. They sat on the ground, facing each other.

"I thought you grew up in a big city," Skeets rattled on. "How did you ever find me?"

"I followed the trail and when it ended I followed the river. It was the only way up. When I got to the summit I found your tracks. It's obvious you were having a hard time finding your way in the midst of that thick cloud just by the marks you left. I trailed you right to the edge."

Skeets marveled at Mr. MacColl's detective work. He was like a seasoned tracker in the woods.

As if sensing that Skeets wondered how he'd found him so easily, Mr. MacColl said, "Because I was a bomber pilot I had to go through intensive survival training in case I ever got shot down, and that included learning to track things, like animals for food, and even humans."

"Even so, it must have been a hard climb for you."

"Was it ever." Mr. MacColl's breathing became steadier. "But I had to find you. I had let you down. I was feeling sorry for myself, making excuses." Mr. MacColl looked hard into Skeets's soft eyes. "I owe you two things, Skeets. An apology. And a thank you."

Shaking his head, Skeets said, "But, Mr. MacColl, I owe you my life. If you hadn't come along I might have never been saved."

Mr. MacColl held up his hand. He took a last big gulp of mountain air. His breathing was now normal. "No, no," he said. "I have to apologize for the crummy way I acted. I had no right to lay my problems on you. Although it sounds weird, I've got to thank you for getting lost up here, because that forced me to put aside my fear of the forest and come look for you."

"But why are you afraid of a few trees and stuff?" Skeets asked. "There's nothing up here that can hurt you." Thinking how he blindly fell off the cliff, he added, "Well, I mean, almost nothing—if you're really careful."

"I'll tell you, Skeets. The last time I was in a forest as dark as this it was in enemy territory. That's when my plane was shot down. I was lucky to survive. Some of my fellow pilots who were shot down were not so lucky. They were either killed or captured and spent years in prison, in the infamous Hanoi Hilton, or were lost forever in the jungles. I was lucky a rescue helicopter found me and got me safely back to the carrier. As you can see, I lost the use of my arm and mangled my leg. I've been feeling sorry for myself ever since. Making excuses for this, making excuses for that. I became a recluse, living in my mother's apartment and hardly ever venturing out. Not until she died."

Mr. MacColl had never made that confession to anyone. Not even his own mother. He found it odd that he was making it to a boy. Yet, he felt better. He felt himself beginning the long journey of putting his demons behind him.

"The reason I owe you," he said, "is that I no longer fear the forest. Climbing up here to find you changed that."

They sat silently for a moment. Then Skeets said, "I have a secret place." He stood up. "Come on, I'll show you." He took a step. The pain in his ankle returned. He limped forward.

Mr. MacColl also got up. He saw Skeets limp. He didn't like the way the boy favored his ankle. "Are you all right?"

"Aw, it's nuthin'. I just turned it when I fell off the cliff."

And then the two limped off into the woods.

14

Mr. MacColl heard the roar of the waterfall before he saw it. Skeets led him through a tangled knot of underbrush and tall pitch pines and Scotch pines and pin oaks and swamp maples. There was no trail. They had to stoop and bend, and slap away sharp branches and thorny vines. They came out on the rim of the waterfall. Below them, black water boiled as if in a granite cauldron.

"This is beautiful," Mr. MacColl said. His voice was almost lost in the din of the waterfall.

Skeets's smile showed how proud he was of this place. And then, slipping out of his sneakers and slipping off his shirt, he jumped off the rim and cannonballed into the churning pool.

Mr. MacColl watched Skeets hit the black water. He hardly made a splash. He sank beneath the roiling surface, and was gone for the longest time. Mr. MacColl was not scared for Skeets. He knew the boy had done this many times. Skeets bobbed to the surface on the far side of the pool, his wet hair flattened against his head. Waving to Mr. MacColl, he signaled for him to jump in.

My last test, Mr. MacColl thought. He stripped off his shirt. An ugly red scar ran the length of his withered arm. Where there should have been muscle there was nothing but skin and bone. He took off his boots. Another scar ran from inside his thigh to below the knee, deep and just as ugly. "Well, here goes nothing." Not allowing himself a second thought, he leaped from the rim.

For fifty feet Mr. MacColl plummeted! He kept his body straight as a javelin. Piercing the black water, he sank to the lowest depths of the pool. The force of the waterfall shoved him downward until his feet touched the rocky bottom. He could not see any light above him, marking the surface. For a split second he feared he was trapped. Maybe the claustrophobia had returned! He wanted to cry out. Instantly, he pushed off—away from the force of the waterfall. The current caught his body and pulled him along and then lifted him up until his head broke out of the water. Sunlight was all around him. But he'd no time to enjoy it. The current kept pushing and pulling him. He was swept over a smaller waterfall and into a less violent pool. His feet scraped bottom. He stood against the current, running his hand over his face, freeing his eyes from so much cold river water so he could see. Skeets sat nearby on a sandy bank. Mr. MacColl limped out of the lower pool. He dropped down next to Skeets.

"That was a gas!" he said. He laughed. Then he wahooed, his voice rising above the roar of the rapids.

Skeets laughed, too. But he couldn't keep his eyes off Mr. MacColl's bum arm.

"Let's do it again!" Mr. MacColl said. He saw Skeets looking at his arm. "It's not pretty, is it? I mean the arm."

"I didn't mean to stare." Skeets looked quickly away. The scar unnerved him.

"Don't feel sorry," Mr. MacColl said. "I'm used to people staring." He ran his good hand over the scar. "This arm was once stronger than the other arm. Now it's as useless as a wet noodle."

"Did it hurt when the plane crashed? I mean when you hit the ground in your parachute?"

Mr. MacColl thought back through the years. He remembered a maimed veteran of the Korean War who'd worked at a corner grocery store in New York's Greenwich Village. He was maybe twenty. He'd been blinded. The thumb and two fingers on his left hand had been blown off. Mr. MacColl was ten years old. He'd gone to the store to pick up a quart of milk for dinner. The sight of the young soldier, his missing eyes and missing fingers, frightened him. He ran out of the store, forgetting the milk.

Mr. MacColl never wanted to be a soldier—an infantryman on the ground. He never wanted to suffer such ghastly wounds. Maybe that's why he'd joined the navy. Perhaps now the sight of his wound frightened Skeets. That was good. War was horrible, and if you could learn that lesson at an early age—then good.

"It didn't hurt at first," he said. "It happened too fast. When the pain came it was unbearable. I wanted to cry out, but I couldn't. The VC, the Vietcong, were on their way to finish the

64

job. I somehow crawled away and climbed up a tree in spite of my wound, and hid among the branches. Later, days later, when they'd left, a navy helicopter sent to rescue me landed and carried me out of the jungle. I was shipped to a military hospital in San Diego. I spent nearly a year there. There was a gal that once loved me, but she couldn't deal with a cripple. . . . Well, that was a long time ago." He got to his feet. "Let's dive into the pool again and ride the rapids!"

Together, they limped back to the pool.

15

All night long Skeets tossed and turned. He couldn't get the adventure atop Catamount Ridge out of his mind. He relived it over and over again, like a rerun on television. Falling off the cliff, miraculously landing on the small ledge, maybe glimpsing the legendary catamount, then saved by Mr. MacColl and seeing the vivid scars on his body. Over and over again.

When his mother banged on the door to awaken him he didn't want to get up.

"Five more minutes, Mom," he begged.

"Now," she said. "Breakfast is ready, and there're chores to do."

Later, at school, Skeets wanted to take a nap. Maybe sneak off somewhere and shut his eyes for a moment or two. Still, he couldn't shake the images of the day before that continually slipped into his mind. But he had something to look forward to, and it kept him going. That afternoon the girls' track team had a meet at home against two high schools—one from New Hampshire and the other from Quebec. He'd have a chance to watch Becky perform, and that he couldn't wait to see.

In class, whenever he thought she wasn't looking, he eyed her. After the last class she walked up to him.

"You are coming to the meet?" she asked, books cradled in her arms.

"Oh, yes," he said, once again feeling blood rush to his head.

"You better." She walked off.

From nowhere an arm circled his head. He felt the tight grip of Emile's muscles. Squirming, he tried to break away. Knuckles scraped his scalp. His entire head burned.

"Gotcha!"

Skeets squirmed some more.

"Got a thing for Becky, do you?" Emile let go with a slight shove. The burning sensation stayed. "I think she's got a thing for you, too." He laughed. He turned and, as he walked away, sniped over his shoulder, "Lovebirds!"

Now Skeets's cheeks burned, and it had nothing to do with the noogie.

The girls' track meet started at three. Most of the members of the boys' team were on hand to support the girls. In the bleachers, Skeets sat next to Billy Abbott. Emile took up a place behind them. Skeets automatically rubbed the top of his head. Emile snickered.

Out on the field and on the track, the girls warmed up. Becky, her hair held back in a ponytail, had been entered in four events—the long jump, 100- and 200-meter sprints, and the 4x100-meter relay. She always ran the anchor leg.

"The team from Canada, Magog High, has a pretty good runner," Billy said. "You ever been up to that end of Memphremagog?"

"Fishin' with my old man and my uncle."

"Me, too. I got family up there, but's too industrialized for me. Magog's got more people living in the city than in our entire Kingdom."

"That's why they always got a pretty good track team," cut in Emile. "Lots of athletes to choose from. But I still beat their best shot-putter last year. And I'll do it again when we meet them tomorrow."

The opening event was the 100-meter dash.

Becky finished her warm-ups. The official called the runners to their marks. Six girls took their places, filling all lanes.

Billy said, "The girl on the inside lane, the lane next to Becky's, with the black ponytail, she's the speedster. Don't know anything about the girls from Colebrook, over in New Hampshire. Should be a tight race." He leaned forward, shouting, "Come on, Becky!"

A tinge of jealousy suddenly swept through Skeets. He didn't like the feeling.

The loud bark from the starter's gun startled Skeets. On the track, Becky broke from the blocks, lunging ahead. The Magog runner got off to a quicker start.

Billy jumped up. "Let's go, Becky! Let's go!"

Skeets jumped up, too.

The girls sprinted neck and neck for the first fifty meters, their spikes soundless on the red synthetic track. Then the Magog runner edged ahead of Becky. Billy and Skeets yelled encouragement. Even Emile stood and shouted, "Pick it up, girl!"

With twenty-five yards to go, it looked like Becky was going to catch her fleet-footed opponent. The two of them were clearly ahead of the rest of the field. One of them was surely going to win.

Skeets's heart pounded against his chest as he pulled for Becky. He bet Billy's heart was pounding, too.

At the finish line, with arms pumping and hair flying, Becky was nosed out.

Skeets's heart sank seeing Becky bent over, her mouth wide open as she gasped for breath, her hands on her thighs. He felt as if he'd run the whole race with her. He slumped down. Billy remained standing, clapping wildly.

"That girl from Magog sure is fast, but so's Becky. She'll catch her in the two hundred. That's 'cause it's a longer race. You watch!"

Becky's next event was the long jump. The Magog girl—they found out her name was Marcelle—was not entered. She was saving herself for the 200 and then the four-by-one-hundred-meter relay, where she'd be running the anchor leg against Becky.

The long jump took some time to complete because of the number of competitors. Each one had three attempts. Becky was the last to jump. At first she loped down the runway. The closer she got to the planting board the faster she went, her legs stretching out in long strides. Then she was off, up in the air. Her legs moved like she was pedaling a fast bicycle. She hit the sand, rolled over, and sprang to her feet. Clumps of sand clung to her calves.

"Mark," snapped the official.

It was the longest jump and she'd won. Up in the stands, Skeets, Billy, Emile—the whole boys' track team—whistled and hooted. Seeing her perform, so graceful as she came down the runway, muscles quivering and then airborne, took away Skeets's breath.

Billy elbowed him in the ribs. "Quite a sight, huh?"

"Yeah," Skeets replied. He tried not to sound too in awe.

"Now she's gotta get revenge on that Canadian girl in the two hundred. It's up next."

Again, all lanes were taken for the 200. Becky and Marcelle were paired in the inside lanes, not quite side by side because the race started on the far curve of the track and the starting marks were staggered. When they came charging around the curve and into the straightaway, then they'd be side by side.

Emile poked his head between Skeets and Billy. "Becky's gonna take her. I can tell just by her body language."

"From that distance?" Billy said.

"Yep!"

Skeets didn't know what to look for as he eyed Becky anew. Was it in the way she moved in front of the starting block? The way she held her head high? The flexing of her arms? He checked her every movement, including the look in her eyes. He also checked the Canadian, Marcelle. What did *her* body language tell him? He couldn't tell the difference between the two rival sprinters, even when they shook hands and then got set. To him they looked friendly enough. When he competed he did it for the pure joy of running, jumping, and throwing. Maybe he didn't have that competitive edge Emile seemed to have. Did Becky have it? He eyed her again in a wholly different way, looking for that one thing that would tell him. He shrugged. If it was there, he couldn't spot it.

"This is gonna be her race," Emile said.

Skeets and Billy swapped glances, each hoping Emile was right.

They were too far from the girls to hear the official. The girls got to their blocks, screwed in their feet, crouched, and waited. The official held the starter's pistol over his head. Skeets saw the puff of the smoke from the barrel before he heard the report.

The girls burst out of the blocks in perfect unison, although it was hard to tell from the ten-meter separation between each sprinter. But the gap closed quickly. As they streaked around the turn for the straightaway, all girls but Marcelle and Becky were running close together. But at the top of the straightaway, in the final ninety meters to the finish line, it turned into a duel between Becky and Marcelle.

The boys were on their feet, stomping and hollering. For Skeets, watching Becky and her rival, their ponytails snapping as they tore down the track, their legs pulling them forward with each savage step and their surprising gracefulness under such stress, caught him off guard. He stopped stomping and hollering, sucked in a lungful of air, and then stood stock-still until the race was over.

The girls flew across the finish line.

"Who won?" Billy yelled. "I can't tell from here."

Skeets had no idea either.

"The Canadian," answered Emile. "Nipped her again."

Like Skeets had done after the 100-meter race, Billy slumped down on the bleacher bench. "Yeah, check out her long legs."

The final two events of the meet were the relays. Magog High won the four by four hundred. The team from Colebrook had grabbed second.

"Another sprint between Becky and the Canadian. Will she win all three of 'em?" a disappointed Billy wondered.

Skeets said nothing. He didn't think he'd get so worked up over a race. Well, he knew why. She was out there on the track.

The first leg was soon under way. The girls, taking up three lanes, churned around the first turn, then handed off the baton to the second leg, then came the third leg. Becky and Marcelle awaited the batons from their teammates before starting the fourth and final leg. The Canadian runner was ahead of Becky's teammate by a stride. Turning her back to the runners racing toward her and Marcelle, Becky began a slow jog, her right arm stretched behind her, left hand open for the baton to be passed to her.

When Becky got the baton, Marcelle was three steps ahead of her.

"No way," grumbled Emile. "No way."

As they came into the final straightaway with Marcelle now running on the inside lane, Becky had gained one step on her. Moving out to the second lane, two steps behind, she lowered her head. Her arms swung back and forth in a blur. Her legs were a blur, too.

"Hot ding-dong!" Billy whooped.

Marcelle seemed to be running out of gas. Three yards from the finish, Becky caught her, flung her head forward, and, nearly stumbling, crossed the line inches in front of the Canadian. Her teammates poured onto the track, cheering, hugging Becky, slapping her on the back.

And Skeets was sure he saw her look his way and a toss a smile aimed just for him.

"Didja see that?" blurted out Billy.

Skeets wondered if maybe Billy thought the smile was for him. Maybe it was. Now it was his turn to slump down in the bleachers.

16

oach Norton deftly twirled his baseball cap in the fingers of his right hand. The top of his balding head shone in the single light of his office. Leaning back in his swivel chair, the desk in his office at the school a mess of papers, he peered over his reading glasses at the best members of his track team. Emile McIntosh, Tommy Patneau, Billy Abbott, and, yes, Skeets Stearns. He'd called them to his office to make an announcement. The four athletes stood in front of their coach, their hands clasped behind their backs.

"Well, boys, I've got good news and bad news," he said. "I'll give it to you straight. You've all qualified to compete in the Boys' Eastern States High School Track and Field Championships next week at Randall's Island in New York City."

The boys murmured among each other. Emile nudged Tommy Patneau with his broad shoulder. Skeets felt a jolt of excitement jump through his body.

Coach raised his hand for quiet. "The bad news is you can't go."

The boys were shocked. "Why?" Emile asked.

"First of all, I can't go," Coach said. "I've got to take our baseball team to the county championship the very day of the track meet. I can't be in two places at the same time. I've decided to go with the baseball team. I owe it to those boys."

"But Coach, what about us?" Emile shot back. "That's not fair."

"Of course it's not fair. Life's not fair. The baseball team has a good shot at the county title. As I just told you, I owe it to them. And you boys can't go alone. You need a coach to be with you. That's the rules." Before they could protest, Coach raised his hand again. "And second," he said, "the school doesn't have the money to send four boys all the way to New York and pay for their hotel and food. It's too expensive. I don't have the funds in my budget to let you go."

"What's it cost?" Skeets asked. "I mean for the four of us to go to New York? I've never been to New York."

"Neither have I," said Emile.

"Me either," added Tommy Patneau.

"I don't rightly know. A couple thousand dollars, maybe twice that. But that's beside the point. You need a coach, and the school doesn't have a coach to spare."

"I think I know someone who'll coach us and take us to New York," Skeets said. "Mr. MacColl. He used to be a track star in New York—that's where he's from. I bet he'd take us."

Coach hadn't thought of Bill MacColl. He knew he'd been a star back in the 1960s. "There's still the problem of money."

"What if we raise the money ourselves?" Emile said.

"How can you raise a couple grand in a week?"

Emile looked at the other boys for help.

"We'll have a town-wide car wash," Billy Abbott said.

"There's not a thousand cars in Hackett's Falls. You'd have to charge five bucks a car to make it worthwhile. That's if everybody wanted their car washed."

"We could hold a bake sale," Tommy Patneau said. "Our moms could bake pies and cakes and cookies and things."

"Let me think it over." Coach was impressed by the eagerness of his track athletes. They'd worked hard all season. He knew they deserved to go. Maybe if the teachers pitched in a few bucks they might raise the money after all.

"Let me ask Mr. MacColl," pleaded Skeets.

Coach nodded. "Tell me what he says."

"Yes sir!" Before he turned to leave, Skeets looked at his coach. "If we go, Coach, what event am I supposed to do at the Easterns?"

"You told me when you came out for the team you wanted to do the decathlon," Coach said, pulling his baseball cap over his head. "So if you go you'll go as a decathlete."

Outside Coach Norton's office, the four athletes huddled.

"New York City," Emile said. "It's a dream come true!"

"We'll be going up against some terrific talent," Tommy

Patneau said. "I mean, terrific!"

"A road trip," said Billy Abbott, squeezing his hands together.

"Hey, we still got money to raise and to see if Mr. MacColl will be our coach," cautioned Skeets. "Then we can get excited."

"Don't be a downer," Emile shot back.

"Hey, look, here comes Becky Winslow," chipped in Billy. "Man she's one good-looking babe."

Becky walked down the hall, with the eyes of Emile, Billy, Tommy, and Skeets on her. As she walked by, she smiled at Skeets. At least, he was sure she did. Maybe she smiled at Billy or maybe Emile, and not at him. She knew he'd been to her track meet, saw her run sprints and long jump. The image of her competing so gracefully was still crystal clear in his mind. *And it always will be,* he thought.

"Hi, Becky." It was Emile talking to her. "We're all going to New York City to compete in a big track meet. Wish us luck."

Becky stopped.

"Yeah," said Billy. "It's exciting. Wish you could come with us."

Becky laughed a sarcastic laugh. "I'm sure you do," she said. "If I went I'd be right there competing next to all of you." She glanced at Skeets. "So, how are you going to get there and where are you going to stay? In the Waldorf Astoria?"

"We haven't figured that out yet," Emile said. "But we will, you can bet on it." He gave Skeets a hard look, making sure he knew it was up to him to convince Mr. MacColl, the cripple with cow dung for brains, to be their coach.

"Well, good luck, you boys," Becky said.

You boys! Skeets swallowed.

"Yeah, well let's go, *you boys*," said Emile, emphasizing "you" with disgust. He and Billy and Tommy started down the hall, looking back once at Becky. Skeets stood still, too frozen to move.

"Hi, Skeets," Becky said. "I saw you at the boys' meet the other day. That was some show you put on."

"Well, I was lucky, is all," he said, swallowing again.

"I also saw you at my meet, sitting up there in the stands. Why'd you show up?"

Skeets turned red, his face burning. All he could do was shrug.

Noticing his embarrassment, Becky reached out and touched his arm. "Well, good luck, then." She smiled, the freckles seeming to jump off her face. "But when you get back I want to hear all about the track meet and how *you* did." She walked off. Skeets watched her go. Every time he was near her he got tongue-tied. He watched her until she disappeared inside the classroom. Why didn't he have the nerve to carry on a decent adult conversation with her?

Oh, I'm such a wimp.

Mr. MacColl was in his room reading *Time and Again* by Jack Finney, a novel about time travel back to New York in the 1890s. He wished he could time travel back to New York to the 1960s and see Kathleen once again. His portable radio was turned to an oldies station. A Beatles tune was playing, "Nowhere Man."

That's me, Mr. MacColl thought, listening to the words. *Nowhere Man.*

At that moment, Skeets pounded on the door.

"Come on in," Mr. MacColl said.

Skeets pushed open the door. "I've got good news and bad news," he said, using the same line as Coach Norton.

"Sounds ominous." Mr. MacColl closed his book and turned down the volume on his radio as the song ended. "What's the problem?"

"Well, four members of the track team have qualified for a meet in New York City. But we can't go. We don't have a coach and we don't have the money!"

"What happened to Coach Norton?"

"He's got to stay here with the baseball team. They're in the county championships. So he can't go. And he said we can't go alone."

"And . . ."

"You can be our coach. Right? I mean, just this one time?"

"Whoa there." Mr. MacColl shifted on his cot. "When's this meet?"

"Next weekend!"

"In the City?"

"You mean New York City?"

Mr. MacColl nodded. "The Big Apple."

"Yes. We've got to earn money so we can stay down there and eat."

Mr. MacColl laughed. "Eat?"

"The school has no money budgeted for this trip. We're going to have car washes and bake sales to raise the money. We need a couple thousand dollars. Maybe more, Coach thinks."

"Where in New York is the meet to be held?"

"I don't know. I think Coach said it's at Randall's Island."

"Randall's Island? I've competed there. Downing Stadium. It's an old concrete stadium almost under the Triborough Bridge. They've had track meets there since way back in the old days. Its first track meet was the 1936 Olympic trials, and the star was the great Jesse Owens. Owens, an African American, then showed up the Nazi athletes in the Olympic Games held in Berlin by winning four gold medals. So Downing Stadium has plenty of history."

"I've never been to New York. None of the guys have. Not even Emile, and we call him the Big Apple."

Mr. MacColl thought about his meets at Downing Stadium. He'd won a couple of decathlons there—including a pair of head-to-head competitions against an old adversary, Bobby Ray Barnes, a self-centered competitor who had miraculously won the silver medal behind the winner, Bill Toomey, at the 1968 Olympic Games in Mexico City, a place where Mr. MacColl should have been. He wondered whatever had happened to Bobby Ray since then. Mr. MacColl now longed to see the old stadium once again, and in his mind's eye relived those two decathlons.

"Okay," he said. "I'll be your coach. Who's going besides you and Emile?"

"Tommy Patneau and Billy Abbott."

"And you don't need to make a lot of money," Mr. MacColl said. "Just bring sleeping bags. The four of you can stay at my mother's apartment in Greenwich Village. It's time I faced that old brownstone and all its memories. I'll drive down. About a couple hundred dollars ought to do it for groceries, gas, and tolls."

"New York City!" blurted a happy Skeets. "The Big Apple!"

17

The trip from the mountains of Hackett's Falls to the skyscrapers of Manhattan was four hundred miles. Driving down Interstate 91 in a beat-up station wagon, Mr. MacColl driving with one arm, took nine hours. Vaulting poles and javelins were strapped to the roof of the station wagon. In the back, sleeping bags and suitcases were crammed in, along with several bags of groceries chipped in by the parents. There wasn't much room for anything else. But crammed in right along with all the gear and groceries, and resting atop the pile, was Tommy Patneau. Skeets and Billy Abbott shared the back seat. Because he was the biggest, Emile McIntosh rode shotgun next to Mr. MacColl. They looked like itinerant workers traveling to their next job.

Everyone was excited, jawing away about their adventure. Skeets was on cloud nine. When they had been packing the station wagon at the school parking lot, Becky showed up to say good-bye and wish them luck. When she came walking toward them, it was Billy who saw her first.

"Look who's coming." He sighed. "It's the one and only Becky Winslow."

Skeets's heart jumped to his throat. Holding a bag of groceries and not moving a single muscle, he watched her cross the parking lot. Holding up her red hair was a green and gold bandanna—the colors of Hackett's Falls High School.

Emile yanked the groceries from Skeets. "Stop gawking like a lovesick puppy," he snapped. "And you, too, Billy."

When Becky reached the station wagon, she smiled. "I just wanted to see *you boys* off," she said. But her smile softened the jibe. "Have a safe trip."

"Let's hurry up and load the wagon," Emile said. He tossed the grocery bags in the wayback.

Becky stood there, arms folded across her chest, as the last of the gear was stowed.

"Fellows, it's time to roll," ordered Mr. MacColl. "It's a long trip down to New York." He got in first. Emile slid into the seat next to him. Tommy climbed into the wayback. Billy got in, darting a peek at Becky. Skeets still stood next to her as if he'd been struck dumb.

"Come on, short stuff," Emile said to him before closing the front passenger door. "Get in, for crying out loud."

Skeets was about to turn away from Becky when she said with some boldness in her voice, "I want you to have this." He looked at her, feeling his heart racing. Becky took the green and gold bandanna from her red hair, shook her head so her hair fell against her slim shoulders, and held it out to him. "Here," she said. "It's a good-luck charm."

Skeets took the bandanna. He clutched it in his fingers, feeling its softness. "Thank you," he mumbled. He didn't know what else to say.

They looked at the ground, their faces red.

"I'll see you when you get back," Becky said.

Skeets hesitated. He felt confused about what to do. And so he only smiled—a stupid, goofy smile, he thought. Then he got into the station wagon and closed the door.

"Are we all set?" Mr. MacColl said, starting the engine.

"Only if lover boy's ready," quipped Emile. He flicked on the radio, turned up the sound. Music blared. Lyrics from the number-one song, by the Police, "Every Breath You Take," filled the station wagon. "Great tune!"

"That's Skeets for sure, watching every move Becky Winslow makes."

Everyone in the station wagon laughed, even Skeets. As the station wagon pulled away from the parking lot, all eyes were on Becky. She looked lonesome, standing there by herself. She waved. Skeets waved through the window. For Mr. MacColl, watching Becky through the rearview mirror brought back a painful memory. He thought of Kathleen Fleming, his long-lost sweetheart. He hummed along with the song. *Every step she takes, I'll be watching her.* He felt as if his heart had broken again.

As the station wagon pulled onto the main road leading out

of the school parking lot, Skeets pressed the bandanna to his face, smelling Becky's fragrance. *Every move she makes.* It was another moment he'd never forget as long as he lived.

Then everyone in the station wagon began to rag on him.

Just south of Saint Johnsbury, Interstate 91 hugged the west bank of the Connecticut River, the boundary between Vermont and New Hampshire. There was little traffic on the highway. It rose and dipped. The valley of the Connecticut River was lush in greenery. Farmland spread every which way. They ate lunch at a Howard Johnson's near Holyoke, Massachusetts.

Skeets had never been to Massachusetts.

"It doesn't look much different than Vermont," he said, chomping on a cheeseburger. He dipped a fry into a puddle of ketchup. "The mountains aren't so high. That's all."

"What mountains?" chortled Emile. "You call those little hills mountains?"

"Once we leave here, we're no longer in the country," Mr. MacColl said. "We'll be driving through what is known as the Northeast Corridor, one of the heaviest concentrations of people in the United States, that stretches from Boston to Washington, D.C. We'll pass through Springfield and Hartford, New Haven, Bridgeport. Combine the populations of some of these cities and they've got more people than the entire state of Vermont."

"Not if you throw in all our cows," quipped Billy Abbott. Everyone laughed.

When they passed through Hartford, the capital of Connecticut, Mr. MacColl announced that it had been the home of Lindy Remigino, a gold medal sprinter in the 1952 Olympics in Finland.

"You'd like his story," he said to Skeets. "Lindy was named after Charles Lindbergh, the first person to fly a plane alone, all by himself, across the Atlantic Ocean. Lindy—Remigino, that is— was not very big. He stood five-six. He was a fast sprinter, but not the fastest in America at the time. But he made the U.S. Olympic team in the one-hundred-meter dash, a huge surprise. Then, not considered to have a chance in the finals of the one hundred, he won by the closest of margins. The first question he asked after crossing the finish was 'Who won?' Replied the judge, 'Why you did, Mr. Remigino.' Then Lindy went over to the guy who was supposed to win, Herb McKenley from Jamaica, and humbly said, 'Gosh, Herb, it looks as though I won the darn thing.'"

Skeets liked the story, and the other boys seemed to as well.

"Connecticut's had a lot of great track champions," Mr. MacColl said. "Two of the most famous are Bill Toomey and Bruce Jenner. Toomey and Jenner won decathlon gold medals. Toomey in Mexico City in 1968. Jenner in Montreal in 1976. What's neat about decathletes is they mostly come from small towns. A few, like me, grow up in big cities. Both Toomey and Jenner were small-town boys from New Canaan and Newtown. Bob Mathias, who won the gold twice, in 1948 and 1952, came from a tiny farming town in California—a lot like Hackett's Falls. He was a year older than you, Skeets, when he won a gold medal. Just seventeen!"

Skeets leaned forward, pressing his elbows on the back of the front seat. He tightly held Becky's bandanna in his right hand. "Why do decathletes come from small towns?"

"My theory is that, in a small town you play all sports. So you become good at a lot of things. Take Emile. He's the star on the football and basketball teams, as well as the track team. If he was from a big town, he might play only one sport.

"When Toomey was competing he'd play mind games with himself. In the hundred meters he'd imagine himself the fastest guy in the world, seeing in his mind's eye his body streaking toward the finish line ahead of everyone. When he'd throw the weights he'd think of himself as strong as anyone and even start talking in a deep, powerful voice as he stepped into the shot put ring."

"That's way too cool," Skeets said. "Has Vermont ever had an Olympic track champion?" Skeets knew his state had plenty of great skiers, like Billy Kidd, Andrea Mead Lawrence, and Barbara Cochran.

"If you've ever been to Burlington, the field house at the University of Vermont is named after Al Gutterson."

"The Gut," everyone said in unison, thinking of the hockey

81

rink at the university. They all followed UVM hockey, both men's and women's.

"Gutterson won the long jump back in 1912! You know who he beat?"

A chorus of noes rang through the station wagon.

Through the rearview mirror, Mr. MacColl looked at the faces of his youthful companions. Perhaps they were not old enough to know the man Gutterson had defeated, but he wanted to see their expressions when he said the name.

"He beat Jim Thorpe." The expressions stayed blank. "Jim Thorpe, the great Indian athlete! Maybe the greatest athlete our country ever had."

"I think I heard of him," Tommy Patneau said from the back of the station wagon. "Didn't he get into some kind of trouble?"

"He did indeed. But it was not his fault."

"What kinda trouble?" Skeets said. He was leaning closer and closer to Mr. MacColl. He loved hearing stories of old-time athletes. In school, his favorite class was history.

"Well, the story of Jim Thorpe begins in the Oklahoma Indian Territory in the late eighteen hundreds. He was born there, mostly a Sac and Fox Indian on his mother's side, with some Irish blood poured in on his father's side. His father taught him to hunt and set traps. And Jim loved to roam. In his teenage years he was a little boy—probably no bigger than you, Skeets. When he was about fifteen, he was sent to the Indian school in Carlisle, Pennsylvania. The coach there was the famous Pop Warner."

"The guy who started Pop Warner Football?" Emile asked.

"Well, he didn't start Pop Warner Football. He was long dead by then. But it was named after him. He was an innovative coach. He invented the huddle. He used to sew fake footballs on the front of his players' uniforms to confuse the defense. He was a wily old guy. Jim was his best player. By the time he was a sophomore at Carlisle Jim had grown into a strong young man, standing over six feet and weighing close to two hundred pounds. He was fast and elusive. He was a three-time All-American football star and a virtual one-man track team. He loved baseball and dropped out of Carlisle for two years to play in the minor leagues in North

Carolina. That was a mistake because, in those days, college players were not allowed to play professional sports. Jim didn't know that. He played for the pure joy of the sport. He made the 1912 U.S. Olympic team. He won the decathlon and the pentathlon—which is like half a decathlon because it's only five events instead of ten."

Skeets felt a prick of pride running through his veins because he was part Native American, like Jim Thorpe, but part Abenaki, not Sac and Fox.

"He also competed in the individual high jump," Mr. MacColl went on, "and the long jump, that was the event Gutterson beat him in, and he played an exhibition baseball game. When the Olympics were over, the King of Sweden placed a crown of laurels on Jim's head and said, 'You, sir, are the world's greatest athlete.' Jim replied, 'Thanks, King.'"

The athletes from Hackett's Falls were spellbound by Mr. MacColl's story about Jim Thorpe. And Mr. MacColl wasn't finished.

"After the Olympics, an enterprising reporter from Worcester, Massachusetts, discovered that Jim had played pro baseball in North Carolina, and spilled the beans with a front-page article. The sporting world got angry. They took away all Jim's medals that he'd won in the Olympics and stripped his name from the record books. And poor Jim, he never knew what happened. He died a pauper. The silver medalist in the decathlon, a Swede named Hugo Wieslander, was declared the winner. Wieslander lived an unhappy life because he knew in his heart of hearts that the true champion was Jim Thorpe. He once came to America to find Jim and give back his medals. But he never found him."

"Did Jim Thorpe *ever* get his medals back?" Skeets wanted to know.

"The International Olympic Committee later decided it had wrongly taken away his medals. They were returned posthumously—long after Jim was dead."

"Do you think he was America's greatest athlete ever?" Billy Abbott asked. "Better than Magic Johnson of the Lakers, or our own Larry Bird of the Celtics? Or how about Ted Williams from the old days, just about the greatest hitter ever?"

"Well, it's hard to say. Times were a lot different back then. Athletes didn't train the way they train today. If you lifted too many weights it was feared you'd get muscle-bound. The tracks were not as fast as they are today. And, of course, diets are better now. But if Jim Thorpe had been born in our age, had all the advantages we enjoy, well, I think he'd surprise all the skeptics who think the world of sports begins and ends with Magic Johnson or Larry Bird or even Darryl Strawberry, the young outfielder for my New York Mets. And don't forget Great Britain's Daley Thompson who's just won two back-to-back Olympic gold medals in the decathlon."

For a long time, no one paid attention to the changing landscape. Skeets had his mind on Becky. Mr. MacColl drove over a concrete bridge and paid a toll. As the station wagon pulled away from the tollgate, the athletes from Hackett's Falls spotted a wide river to their right. On the far side it was rimmed with high bluffs.

"That's the Hudson River," he told them. "And the cliffs across the river in New Jersey are the Palisades." The station wagon followed the highway down a long, curving slope. The highway then straightened out. "Just ahead is the George Washington Bridge."

The mighty bridge towered above the Hudson. It had two levels to handle all the traffic pouring back and forth across the river.

"Welcome to New York City!" Mr. MacColl said.

"We're really here!" Skeets pushed his face against the window. "Where's the Empire State Building? Yankee Stadium?"

"The only thing you'll see today is the Empire State Building. We're on the West Side Highway. I'll drive down Broadway, then over to Fifth Avenue. You'll get to see the heart of Manhattan!"

As he spoke, the station wagon passed under the George Washington Bridge. Everyone craned upward to look at the underbelly of the giant span. On the Hudson River huge oil tankers and barges and sleek sailboats moved with the current.

"Look to your left," ordered Mr. MacColl. "Up on the hill, do you see that round white structure? That's the tomb of U. S.

Grant, the Civil War general and president of the United States." He paused, then asked with a smile, "Who's buried in Grant's tomb?"

"Who?" Emile said.

"Why, Grant, of course."

Everyone groaned.

Skeets was more interested in the tall buildings. There were so many and they were so big, clawing at the sky. Skyscrapers, all right! It looked as if there wasn't an inch of ground where a tree or a bush might grow. How could people live in such a place? He saw why Mr. MacColl had described the city as claustrophobic.

Mr. MacColl exited the West Side Highway. Traffic loomed all around them. Horns blared constantly. He drove crosstown to Broadway and Times Square. Although it was late afternoon, neon lights brought thousands of signs to life. Marquees advertised the latest movies and plays. One whole building had a baseball player painted on its side. Traffic crawled. To the surprise of Skeets, bicyclists shot through the traffic at breakneck speed. People jostled each other on the crowded sidewalks. They darted across the street, slipping in between cars and taxis and trucks as deftly as any athlete. Skeets had never seen people walk so fast. Meanwhile, vendors hawked their wares at small tables lining the edge of the sidewalk. And amid all the confusion, curled up in doorways, hoping to pick up some spare change, were dirty, ragged homeless people.

The scene never changed. The hustle and bustle and noise were endless. It seemed to Skeets that in New York City confusion reigned.

"Look up," Mr. MacColl said. Once again, the boys craned upward. "We're passing by the Empire State Building, at one time the world's tallest building."

"This is where King Kong got it, isn't it?" hollered Tommy Patneau from the wayback.

"That's right!"

The Empire State Building looked as high as Catamount Ridge.

After a bit, they saw ahead of them an arch crossing the street.

Anticipating their next question, Mr. MacColl announced that the arch marked the entrance to Washington Square Park. "Welcome to Greenwich Village, my hometown!"

The street they were on was Fifth Avenue. It ended at the arch. Mr. MacColl turned right, skirting the edge of the park. He wove in and out of a number of skinny side streets. And then stopped.

"Here we are," he said. "The house of my childhood." The building he nodded to was a brownstone. A stoop ran up to a heavy door with a lot of brass and glass. Long windows with wide wooden sashes that were in need of paint decorated the front. The building looked like all the others on the street.

"Where you gonna park?" asked Billy Abbott. From one corner of the street to the other, on both sides, every parking space was filled.

"I'll find a spot. But, in the meantime—everybody out!"

The boys piled out of the station wagon. They were stiff from the long trip down from the mountains of northern Vermont. They stretched themselves. They took out their luggage, sleeping bags, and groceries and put them on the sidewalk while Mr. MacColl drove off to find a place to park. To Skeets's surprise, the street was quiet. It was not as crowded as the others he'd seen. The few people on the sidewalk did not rush past. They ambled, taking their time and nodding to the boys as they went. After all, this was their neighborhood.

Mr. MacColl came limping up the sidewalk. "Let's go inside and hope there's not a lot of dust in the old apartment," he said, leading the boys up the stoop. "It's been empty now for a couple of months." Unlocking the door, he felt a tinge of sadness. It had been four months since his mother had died.

It was a surprisingly small place, Skeets thought. It looked like it had two living rooms, each with a marble fireplace. Both living rooms were long, but not too wide. He walked to the front room that overlooked the street. The windows reached to the floor. They were like glass doors. On the outside were steel bars. It felt like he was standing inside a jail cell.

He went to the mantel over the fireplace where a row of

photographs was displayed. One photograph in a gilt-edged frame showed a woman and two men. Skeets recognized one of the men, Mr. MacColl. He looked so different. He was young and muscular, and in a track uniform. All three were smiling into the camera. Skeets looked at the arm that had been ruined in the war. There was no awful red scar. The muscles looked hard and strong. Another photograph revealed Mr. MacColl in his dress-white navy uniform. Next to the photograph were two ribbons with medals dangling from them. One was purple in the shape of a heart. Skeets picked it up. In the center of the heart was a gold bust of George Washington. He rubbed the face of Washington, knowing the medal had to be a big deal, then put it back on the mantel. He picked up the other ribbon. It was red, white, and blue. The medal was bronze with a four-bladed propeller in the shape of a cross etched onto it.

Mr. MacColl, who'd been watching Skeets, said, "That's the Distinguished Flying Cross. Just a cheap piece of metal. Now let's bring in the groceries and see if we can rustle up some food."

18

Randall's Island seemed the most unlikely place for a sporting event. At least it did to the troop of wide-eyed Vermonters. Wedged between the East and Harlem rivers, it was a sliver of land underneath a maze of twisting concrete, four-lane highways, and steel railroad tracks. Randall's Island was home to Downing Stadium. The stadium was made of chipped and crumbling concrete, over fifty years old. Stepping through the dark, gloomy entrance and hiking up a flight of cold, clammy stairs to the stands, the Hackett's Falls contingent felt they'd stepped back in time. Like the book Mr. MacColl had been reading, Skeets thought, *Time and Again.* To lend an aura of age, old-time photographs of great track stars adorned dank, dimly lit walls. Inside Downing Stadium, the brick-red track that encircled grass as green as any Skeets or Emile or Billy or Tommy had ever seen was the only indication that a meet was taking place in the 1980s, not back in the dark ages of the twentieth century. The glistening track was eight lanes wide. The track at Hackett's Falls was a skimpy six lanes and in rough condition.

Skeets couldn't wait to run on this track.

"Wow!" Emile said.

Dozens of high school teams were already in the stands. Many of the teams had erected tarpaulin shelters to shield their athletes from the sun. On the track and field below, young athletes from all over the East Coast warmed up. At the open end of the stadium, huge tents marked where officials and scorekeepers gathered, and where hot dogs and hamburgers and soft drinks were sold.

"*Holy wow,*" Emile said.

Mr. MacColl surveyed the familiar scene. He hadn't been inside Downing Stadium since he'd been competing as a senior at New York University. He felt the excitement of the track meet rising in his breast—as if he was about to tackle the decathlon himself. He placed his good arm across Skeets's shoulder, but said to everyone, "For the next two days you're going to have the time of your lives. Remember it always!"

Skeets looked up at Mr. MacColl. He then looked back at all the athletes. He saw banners from cities and towns he'd barely heard of—Poughkeepsie, Schenectady, and Skaneateles, New York; Great Neck and Centereach, Long Island; Perth Amboy, New Jersey; Baltimore, Maryland; Caribou, Maine; Youngstown, Ohio; Altoona, Aliquippa, and York, Pennsylvania; Coventry, Rhode Island; Winchester, Virginia; and Wheeling, West Virginia. Big cities like Boston and Concord and Richmond, as well as the Big Apple itself. And, of course, little places like Hackett's Falls.

Mr. MacColl unfurled a green and gold banner that displayed a magnificent mountain lion pawing the air. Below, it read: "Hackett's Falls Regional High School, Vermont, Home of the Catamounts!" Skeets recognized it as the banner that hung inside the school gym. *Catamounts!* The same nickname as the University of Vermont.

"Coach Norton gave this to me before we left," Mr. MacColl told his squad. He saw the pride in his small group of athletes. He was happy he'd thought to bring it along.

Eagerly, the excited representatives from Vermont's sparse North Country put up their banner and tarp, as Mr. MacColl checked his watch. It was 9 a.m. The meet didn't officially start until ten. According to the schedule of events, there was to be an opening ceremony, a parade of athletes once around the track, proudly holding their banners like in the Olympics. Then came the first event of the decathlon.

"I want you fellows to warm up," he said. "Tommy," he added, pointing south to the open end of Downing Stadium, "there's the pole vault runway. The vault isn't supposed to start until noon. But get familiar with it. It's tricky, especially if we get a swirling crosswind."

Tommy picked up his poles, balanced them on his shoulder, and picked his way out of the stands.

Mr. MacColl watched Emile, Billy, and Skeets head toward the track. Being a coach had never crossed his mind. Now that he'd been forced into it—well, not really forced—he liked the thought.

He did have something to offer the world after all.

Skeets loped slowly around the track, running next to Emile. There were so many athletes crowded onto the track, like a circus.

"I bet there're guys here who can throw the shot sixty feet!" Emile said.

Skeets looked around, still amazed at the number of high school athletes. There were probably more people crowded on the track and field than lived in all of Hackett's Falls. And many of them were African American. There was not a single Black family living in Hackett's Falls. Black people lived in Burlington, but he hardly got over there. He saw Asians, too, and Latinos.

"Look at the size of that guy," Emile said. They ran past a Black athlete who stood at least six feet six inches. His arms were thick as logs. "That's no teenager."

Skeets had to agree. Maybe he was a coach. But then, why was he warming up? His sweat suit read Overbrook High School.

"I bet he's a shot-putter," Emile said, defeat tolling in his voice.

A voice crackled from a loudspeaker. "All athletes assemble at the open end of Downing Stadium for the opening ceremonies and parade."

"We need our banner," Skeets said. He dashed up into the stands. Mr. MacColl had already taken it down. As Skeets took it from him, he said, "There's a Black kid down there who looks like a man."

"Well, I bet he's only a year or two older than you, if that, but if he's been living in Philadelphia's inner city," Mr. MacColl said, noting the boy's sweat suit, "I'll bet he's already lived a lifetime."

Skeets went back down onto the field and crossed over to the open end of the stadium. There he met Billy and Tommy and Emile.

"A lady told us we're to line up alphabetically by state," Billy said.

"That means we're last, as usual," Emile said.

"Not this time," Tommy said. "I think Virginia and West Virginia are behind us."

The four athletes went to the rear of the throng. They saw

other high schools from Vermont. Burlington had two schools represented. Barre, Bennington, Brattleboro, Montpelier, and Rutland, all the big cities were there. Some had only one athlete, others two or three.

"Guess what?" Emile said. "We're the only hick school from Vermont. Maybe in the entire stadium!"

"Then that makes us special," Skeets said.

They took their place. Each one held a piece of the banner. Emile and Tommy were on the inside, flanked by Billy on the left and Skeets on the right. Soon they were marching around the track. The announcer read the names of all the high schools as they passed by the grandstand. Spectators cheered them all, as if there were no favorites. The grandstand was draped in red, white, and blue bunting, like at the World Series. Dignitaries stood and clapped as the schools marched by. It reminded Skeets of the Olympics. When all the schools were on the track, they halted. "The Star-Spangled Banner" was played. Then a man identified as the mayor of New York ordered the Boys' Eastern States High School Track and Field Championship officially opened. Everyone cheered.

In the stands once again, Skeets and Emile rehung their banner.

"How's your ankle?" Mr. MacColl asked. He'd taped it back at the apartment.

"It's fine," Skeets said.

The loudspeaker crackled again. "Ladies and gentlemen, in about fifteen minutes the first event of the day will begin. The decathlon one-hundred-meter dash. There are seventeen decathletes entered in the competition. I'd like to draw your attention to one of the decathletes. Representing King School from East Neck, Long Island, and last year's national champion, Bobby Ray Barnes Jr."

Mr. MacColl's head jerked up at the sound of the name. Skeets saw him stand quickly, twisting his body, searching the stands. He tried to follow Mr. MacColl's eyes.

"If the name sounds familiar—it should," the announcer continued. "Bobby is the son of two-time U.S. Olympian and

1968 Olympic silver medalist Bobby Ray Barnes. Mr. Barnes is here with us today. Let's give him and his son a hearty New York City welcome!"

From the far end of the stadium, near the vaulting pit, a big man with silver hair rose and waved as the crowd politely clapped. Skeets watched Mr. MacColl stare at the man. His face was set as hard as steel. The muscles along his jaw twitched. At that moment, Skeets heard Mr. MacColl mutter, "At long last we meet again." Turning to Skeets, he said, "You better get down on the field and warm up for the one hundred."

As Skeets started down the stands toward the track, Mr. MacColl grabbed his shoulder. He felt his grip like iron, pinching him. "I've always told you to do your best—no matter what. And I want you to do that today. But I want you to do something else," he said. "I want you to beat the Barnes kid."

Then he let go of Skeets's shoulder.

19

Only thirteen decathletes showed up—not seventeen. *An unlucky omen*, Skeets thought. And one of them was the towering Black athlete from Philadelphia. Shaved into the short curly hair on the back of his head was the word DECA. Skeets had seen such haircuts on MTV. Nobody wore them around Hackett's Falls. Emile didn't have to worry about the big athlete after all, because he wasn't in the individual shot put. But now Skeets had to worry.

Sitting on the track, Skeets stretched his legs in preparation for the 100-meter dash. As he reached out to touch the toes of his left foot, he saw the kid striding his way. The kid's feet were enormous.

He squatted next to Skeets. "Can you pole-vault?" he asked. He had a deep man's voice and the wondering eyes of a teenager.

"A little," said Skeets, trying not to stare at the size of his hands.

"Me, too. I've done ten feet once. But I don't like what can happen once you leave the ground and turn upside down. Scary, isn't it?"

Skeets had never thought pole-vaulting to be scary. "I guess."

The kid stuck out his huge hand, a paw really, as big as a bear's. "I'm Robinson James, from Philly. The City of Brotherly Love. I'm a junior at Overbrook High, the same school Wilt Chamberlain went to."

Skeets shook the big hand, noticing how puny his was in comparison. "I'm Skeets Stearns, from Hackett's Falls, that's way up in Vermont by the Canadian border," he said. "Who's Wilt Chamberlain?"

"Just about the greatest basketball player ever. He scored a hundred points in a single NBA game. I've never been to Vermont. Lots of trees up there?"

"You bet," Skeets said.

"Any Indians still living up there?" Robinson smiled.

"Yeah," Skeets replied. "A few of us."

"Us?"

"On my mom's side I've got plenty of Abenaki blood in me."

"No kidding." Robinson gave Skeets a surprised second look, and smiled again. "I've never met an Indian before, or should I call you a Native American?"

"Makes no difference to me."

"Skeets? Is that an Indian name?"

"Nope. It's a nickname my uncle gave me. Short for Skeeter."

Robinson nodded. "Like in mis-skeeters?"

Skeets laughed. "You have a first name for a last name and a last name for a first name."

"I do. My parents named me for the baseball player Jackie Robinson and gave me the middle name of Jesse after the great Olympic runner Jesse Owens, not the outlaw Jesse James. Jesse Owens showed up the Nazis at the 1936 games in Berlin, Germany. And Jackie Robinson was the first Black guy to play in the major leagues. He was an infielder for the old Brooklyn Dodgers, back like a million years ago, in the nineteen forties and fifties. He mostly played second base."

"My coach told me about him—he likes sports history, tells us a lot of stuff about old-time athletes. I like hearing about guys like Robinson and Jim Thorpe."

"I heard of Jim Thorpe. My coach said he was about the best there ever was." Then Robinson asked, "Have you ever done a decathlon before?"

"No. I'm new at this stuff."

"Well, I've done one," Robinson said. "Last year. I came in fourth. My coach thinks I can finish second this year behind Bobby Ray—if I can get past the pole vault. I love the decathlon. Everyone back in Philly wants me to concentrate on basketball, but I'd rather run and jump and throw things around. More fun."

"But isn't that a lot like basketball? Running and jumping, shooting basketballs at a hoop?"

"Yeah, but this is still more fun."

As they talked, a decathlete loped past them. He was in a red, white, and blue warm-up suit. He was about six-one and 185 pounds, his blond hair cut short on the sides, but long and tapered in the back like a rat's tail. He moved with a grace that both Skeets and Robinson couldn't help but admire. Stitched loudly on his chest was *The King*, and the name of his school.

"That's the guy who's gonna win," Robinson said. "Bobby Ray Barnes. His father was an Olympic hero."

So that's Barnes, Skeets thought, *and Mr. MacColl wants me to beat him!*

As Skeets and Robinson warmed up together, practicing their starts, sprinting ten and twenty yards, Bobby Ray stood apart. He talked to no one. He didn't even nod an acknowledgment to the others in the competition. At last year's championship, he'd won the decathlon by almost five hundred points, scoring 7,176 points. It was among the highest totals in high school history. Every major college courted him. *Sports Illustrated* ran a feature on him at the beginning of the season, "The Prep School Phenom." He was nearly as famous as his father.

Skeets wondered why Mr. MacColl wanted him to beat Bobby Ray. That was crazy. He'd never have a chance. It wasn't just that he was small. He wasn't close to being *that* good. Not by a mile. Not ever!

When the heats and lane assignments were issued, Skeets found himself in the first heat—along with Robinson and Bobby Ray, and a New Yorker from Albany named Andy Van Buren. Andy smiled a lot and twitched his shoulders, and rubbed his hands constantly. The four stood before the metal starting blocks. They shook hands all around, except for Bobby Ray. The official starter came up. He wore a white baseball cap and a red armband. In his right hand he held a pistol. It was connected to a long wire that snaked out behind him onto the infield grass.

"Listen up, gentlemen," he said. "I'm going to say 'on your marks' and then 'set,' and the gun will go off. You each get one false start, and then you're disqualified from the race. So listen to me carefully."

The four decathletes knelt along the starting line. "On your marks!"

95

The four decathletes screwed their feet into the starting blocks.

Getting ready, Skeets realized he'd never run a 100-meter race before. He looked to his left. Robinson stared straight ahead, his mouth a straight line of determination. He looked to his right. Bobby Ray had the same look as Robinson. On Bobby Ray's right, Andy twitched his shoulders once and then grew perfectly still. Skeets looked down the length of the track. The lanes, marked in white chalk, converged in the distance like railroad tracks. It was only a footrace, he told himself. But he felt a knot tighten in his stomach as hard as stone.

"Set!"

The four decathletes rose in unison to the balls of their feet. Their hands pressed on the track for balance. They leaned forward, like tightly wound coils. Skeets felt his throat go dry.

The starter's gun erupted like a cherry bomb, and a cloud of smoke spat from its barrel.

Skeets was amazed at how fast Robinson and Bobby Ray broke from the starting blocks. Their feet thundered on the track like horses. They were already a full body length in front of him. And they hadn't gone five meters. Skeets reached out with his short legs, lifting them up and setting them down as fast as he could—straining with all his might. Yells from the stands urged them all forward. As hard as he tried, he couldn't catch any of the runners. Their long legs pulled them further and further ahead. They barged over the finish line, with Skeets last in his heat.

"Stay in your lanes," an official hollered.

As Skeets gasped for air, his dry throat aflame, disappointment swept over him like a wave. He'd run so hard and so fast, and yet finished last! Keeping his head down, he avoided Robinson's shining, dark eyes.

The electric timer, stationed at the finish line, flashed the winning time. It was 11.28 seconds. Skeets had no idea who'd won. Most likely Bobby Ray. He was so far behind, he probably ran at least two seconds slower. What a great start to his first decathlon.

Robinson came over, breathing hard, and offered his hand. Skeets shook it, but still avoided his eyes.

Andy slapped him on the back. "What a race!" Andy said between gulps of air. "We were all so close." He twitched his shoulders.

"I think you beat us," Robinson said.

"I dunno," Andy said. "Bobby Ray was with me all the way."

At the mention of Bobby Ray, Skeets turned. Bobby Ray was walking off the track. He hadn't bothered to congratulate anyone. When all the times were posted, Andy had indeed won at 11.28. Bobby Ray was second at 11.32, Robinson was third at 11.44, and Skeets fourth at 11.76. As it turned out, after all the heats were run, Andy's time stood as the fastest among the thirteen decathletes. Bobby Ray's was still second. But Robinson's time dropped him to sixth, and Skeets's to ninth.

Andy collected 799 points, Bobby Ray 791, Robinson 765, and Skeets 699.

Skeets didn't know if he was off to a good start in the decathlon—after all, he was in ninth place. He remembered Mr. MacColl telling him that to win a decathlon you didn't need to capture every event. In fact, he'd said you could win the whole thing without winning a single event. It still seemed an odd way to be a champ, he thought, as he and Robinson and Andy walked toward the long jump pit at the west end of Downing Stadium.

20

Tommy Patneau was near the long jump runway that ran parallel with the pole vault runway. He was squatting on his haunches, one of his vaulting poles propped against his shoulder.

"Hi, Tommy," Skeets said. "When do you start jumping?"

"Not till noon."

Tommy eyed Robinson. He made Emile McIntosh, the Big Apple, look like a grape.

"This is Robinson James and Andy Van Buren. They're both in the decathlon." Tommy shook their hands. "Where's the big star?" he asked. "The kid whose father was an Olympian? They sure made a big deal out of him."

Robinson nodded toward Bobby Ray, who'd set up an umbrella near the long jump pit and was settling under it. "That's the man."

"I hear he's a good vaulter," Tommy said.

"I saw him clear sixteen feet at an indoor meet at Madison Square Garden this winter," Robinson said.

"Madison Square Garden!" Skeets said. To hear Robinson mention the great New York sports arena excited him. He didn't think high schools ever competed there. It was only for college and pro teams. He thought what a thrill it must be to compete in such a legendary place. Robinson smiled as if he knew what was going on in Skeets's mind.

Then Andy cut in, twitching his shoulders. "My coach says Bobby Ray is, like, ranked fifth in the nation in the pole vault. That's his event, for sure. At the Empire State Games last year in Syracuse, I saw him win with a jump of sixteen-four. He'll be clearing eighteen feet soon as he gets to college."

"I hear he's signed a letter of intent to go to either the University of Tennessee, Arkansas, or Southern California. One of those big track schools," Robinson said.

"USC," Andy said. "His old man wants him out in the sunny West where he can train year-round. He's grooming him for the Olympics. I read that in the *Sports Illustrated* article."

"Bobby Ray's good, all right," Robinson said. "But I wonder how tough he'd be if he ever found himself in a tight spot."

"He'd have a good excuse, you can bet on it," Andy said.

A half hour later, after all the decathletes had warmed up, the long jump got under way. The runway at the stadium's south end paralleled the pole vault runway. There were no heats, but the order was the same.

Andy led off. Streaking down the runway, he launched himself high into the air—his arms and legs flailing away like a windmill. He landed in a spray of sand.

"Mark!" hollered an official, holding up a white flag.

Andy's jump measured 6.78 meters—twenty-two feet three inches. It scored 762 points. He raised his fist in exaltation. He and Robinson high-fived each other. Turning to Skeets, he said, "I can't believe it. I just beat my best jump by a foot!"

Bobby Ray was next. He slowly came out from under his umbrella and shed his warm-up suit. Skeets admitted to himself that Bobby Ray looked and acted like a great athlete, and if what everyone said about him was true, then he probably was headed straight for fame. He studied the Long Island youth as he trotted to the head of the runway. Bobby Ray touched the ground with the palms of his hands, flexed both legs, and straightened out. He glared down the runway with a fierce intensity that clearly showed on his face. He rocked back and forth, then sprang forward. He gathered momentum with each step. He snapped his right foot down on the planting board and took off. His form was perfect, or at least looked perfect to Skeets, who'd never long-jumped before. He guessed Bobby Ray had done it right. His leap was 6.72 meters—twenty-two feet one inch. It was shorter than Andy's by two inches. Bobby Ray earned 750 points. After his jump, he showed no emotion. He went back under his umbrella, shunning the others.

Robinson followed Bobby Ray. The tall, strong youth from Philadelphia, his long legs propelling him down the runway like a locomotive, reached 6.57 meters, not quite twenty-one feet seven inches. He picked up 713 points.

And then it was Skeets's turn. Looking down the runway, he felt everyone in Downing Stadium had their eyes pasted on him. He shuffled back and forth, drawing his breath in deep, even gasps. Then, holding his breath like he was swimming underwater, he took off. His feet pounded lightly on the runway. Each step drew him closer to the planting board. The board was in front of him sooner than he expected. He hit it and sprang upward. When he came down and rolled over in the gritty sand, he heard the official yell "Foul!" and spotted him holding up a red flag. The jump didn't count!

The first to greet him was Robinson. He patted Skeets on his small but strong shoulders. "Don't worry. You got two more jumps. Adjust your steps, that's all. You'll do fine next time."

Skeets wasn't so sure. He had to wait nearly twenty minutes before his second jump. Neither Andy nor Bobby Ray nor Robinson bettered their first jumps.

As he got ready for his second try, Skeets worried about his timing. All he wanted to do was hit the planting board perfectly. He broke down the runway, watching for the board. But when it loomed in front of him, he realized too late that his steps were still out of sync. He slowed down, hit the board squarely, and lifted off. In the air, he strained to hear the official. But there was only stillness. He sank into the sand and sprawled forward, headfirst.

"Mark!" snapped the official, holding up the white flag.

Skeets's jump was 5.64 meters—eighteen feet six inches. He slumped onto the grass, dejected. How could a long jump be so hard? It seemed so simple. Run fast and jump. That's all there was to it, right? But for that darn planting board. It was as hard to hit as that Pesky Pole at Boston's Fenway Park that he'd seen on TV.

This time Robinson and Andy didn't talk to him. They didn't want to jinx him on his last try.

Once again, Skeets had to wait a long time. Meanwhile, no one matched their first efforts. Andy still had the best jump, followed by Bobby Ray and Steve O'Grady, a boy from Boston, who'd reached 6.65 meters—twenty-one feet ten inches.

Collecting his thoughts at the top of the runway, Skeets tried to visualize himself on Catamount Ridge. He closed his eyes and saw the thick forest all around him. He saw the gorge, white water tumbling over it in a roar of immense hydropower. And then he was like the mountain lion, racing perilously close to the edge. He could hear padded paws pounding against the ground. And there, opening his eyes—just ahead—was the planting board, shining like glass in the sun. He struck it and was in the air! He sailed on, arms and legs pumping wildly.

"Mark," snapped the official once again.

Dusting himself off, Skeets strained to hear his measurement.

"Six meters fifty-five."

It was a twenty-one-foot-six-inch jump. As it turned out, it was the fifth-best jump of the day. Skeets rolled out of the pit, flecks of sand stuck to his sweaty body. He wiped himself off. And when he couldn't shake the image of himself as a mountain lion, he smiled.

21

The shot put was the first chance for the stronger boys to score a lot of points.

For Robinson it was time to shine. The shot put was his specialty. Andy knew his early lead in the ten-eventer was over. He didn't have the strength. Bobby Ray didn't expect to win, yet he knew there weren't many decathletes who tossed the shot farther. And Skeets, who'd practiced putting a few times with Mr. MacColl behind the family barn, figured ten meters was all he was going to get.

Meanwhile, other events were just getting started on the track. Competitors for the 100-meter dash were limbering up.

The shot put ring was on the grass in the middle of Downing Stadium. Andy, now used to starting first, twitched his shoulders, got into the ring, crouched, skipped forward with two quick steps, and heaved the twelve-pound iron orb. It sailed a short way. When his toss was measured, it was 8.90 meters, barely twenty-nine feet.

Bobby Ray took his time. He hefted the iron ball in his right arm high over his head. The muscles in his shoulder rippled. Like Andy, he crouched. But instead of gliding across the ring, he spun like he was throwing the discus. Skeets had never seen the shot putted in that style. With his last spin Bobby Ray roared. His voice echoed inside the stadium. The shot sailed upward then thudded into the soft turf. His effort reached 13.42 meters—forty-four feet.

Pleased with his toss, he strutted out of the back of the ring. The strut didn't bother Robinson. He'd seen it often enough on the playgrounds of Philadelphia. Picking up the shot in his huge hands, he turned to Andy and Skeets. "I think I'm gonna show that *boy* a thing or two."

Like Bobby Ray he raised his right arm. His muscles were more pronounced than Bobby Ray's. He dropped quickly into his crouch. Swiftly he was across the ring. In his mind, Skeets could hear Mr. MacColl explaining to him and Emile about speed, about explosiveness. Robinson's shot went airborne. It was like mortar shot from a cannon. It rose higher and sailed farther than Bobby Ray's toss.

"Fourteen meters twenty-five," bellowed the official.

Robinson slapped his hands together. There was no way Skeets could come close to either Robinson or Bobby Ray. Mr. MacColl wanted ten meters. Anything less would be a disappointment.

Standing in the rear of the ring, he looked across the infield to the stands. He saw the Hackett's Falls banner. He saw Mr. MacColl standing, looking back at him. As he crouched, he tried to remember all the things he'd been taught. Keep low, glide fast, and spring upward—all in a single, fluid motion. Be explosive! He got low, like he was told, slid across the ring with great force, and shot upward—off his feet. The iron orb came off his hands like a rocket launcher. He stood watching it travel away from him. Its distance startled him. When it pounded into the ground, he realized it'd gone almost as far as Bobby Ray's toss!

Skeets leaped out of the front of the ring. With his fist shot gloriously in the air, he danced about.

"Foul," shouted the official.

Skeets stopped his dance. He felt his heart leap to his throat. *Foul!*

"Why? Whatta I do wrong?"

"You're not allowed to exit the front of the throwing circle," the official told him. "Only the rear. You should know that."

"But I didn't know! Nobody told me."

"Your coach should've taught you better. Sorry, son. You'll know next time."

"But my coach never told me!" Skeets's blood began to boil.

"Well, that's what you get for a having a coach from one of those one-horse towns up in Vermont."

"He's not from Vermont. He's from New York." He spat out the words. "He's Bill MacColl!"

"Never heard of him. Like I said, son, he should've known."

Skeets snatched up his shot. He walked past the umbrella that shielded Bobby Ray from the hot sun, angry with himself, angry with Mr. MacColl, and disappointed that his great throw didn't count.

From under the umbrella, Bobby Ray broke his silence.

"Hey, you, from the one-horse town." The sound of his cold voice, icily coming from the shadows of the umbrella, caught Skeets off guard. It was the first time he'd heard anything uttered by Bobby Ray to anyone. "That coach of yours wouldn't by any chance be Bill MacColl from my dad's era? My dad told me stories about their decathlon duels. Them and Bill Toomey. He only beat my dad once. Probably the officials were on his side."

Skeets slowed down. "I think it's the same Bill MacColl. Why?"

"I bet my dad would like to know. And the official's right, by the way. MacColl should have known better."

A seething Skeets slumped down next to Robinson and Andy. Robinson was thumbing through a little blue book. In fact, its title was *Little Blue Book*.

Hugging his knees, Skeets allowed his head to hang down. "Why didn't I know about that dumb rule?" he snapped.

"Lift your head up," Andy said. "You've got two more tosses."

"Look at this," Robinson said, holding out the blue book. "I got 744 points for my throw."

Skeets looked at the book. Page after page was filled with numbers.

"What kinda book is this?" he asked, still smarting from his foul in the shot put. *No—MacColl's foul!*

"It's the scoring tables for the decathlon," Robinson said. "See, under the shot, it has the distance in both feet and meters, and next to it the number of points you get. My toss was fourteen meters twenty-five. That's 744 points. If I don't improve on my next two throws, I'll have scored a total of 2,222 points after three events. Now, if Bobby Ray doesn't improve, I'll be ahead by fourteen points." Then Robinson sighed. "But then it's all downhill. I'll probably beat him in the discus and maybe the javelin. But that's it. Unless something happens, he ought to win this thing going away."

Robinson did not improve on his first toss. Bobby Ray did, reaching 13.21 meters, or a quarter inch over forty-three feet four inches. It gave him 680 points and put him only a single point behind Robinson: 2,222 to 2,221.

Andy never reached ten meters. And after three events, he dropped in the standings from first to third with 2,045 points.

Skeets failed to match his first effort. He was tentative in the ring, afraid to make another error. On his last throw, he got the shot past ten meters, barely. He picked up 489 points. He was in ninth place with 1,897 points.

The high jump took place at the north end of Downing Stadium, opposite the long jump. As the decathletes trudged past the stands, Skeets spotted Mr. MacColl beckoning to him. He hiked into the stands.

"How are you feeling?" he asked. "You got that hangdog look."

"I made a terrible mistake in the shot put. I walked out of the front of the ring and not the back. I didn't know any better. How come you didn't tell me?"

"My fault," Mr. MacColl said. "I didn't explain all the rules to you. I'm sorry for that. But you're still not out of it, yet. So lift your head up!" He squeezed Skeets's shoulders in a reassuring way.

"But Robinson James told me I lost about two hundred points because I stepped out the wrong end."

Mr. MacColl flinched when he heard the angry disappointment in Skeets's voice. "You can't worry about what might have happened. Remember, we wanted ten meters. And we got that, didn't we?"

"Yes sir. But—"

"But no excuses. Put the shot behind you. The only thing you think about now is the high jump. Your steps, your approach, arching your back, and snapping your legs up. *Power! Power! Power!* All in a fluid motion. And we want six feet. I know you can do six feet in your sleep. Up on Catamount Ridge, I watched you jump over logs like nothing. Six feet. Okay?"

Skeets trotted down to the high jump area. *No excuses,* he said to himself, and his anger began to dry up. The other decathletes were warming up, except Bobby Ray. Skeets looked for him. He was in the stands, talking to his famous father. They were looking toward the Hackett's Falls banner. Bobby Ray's father was holding his hand over his eyes, shielding them from the bright sunlight as he searched for MacColl.

22

The opening height was five feet four inches. Not all the decathletes entered at that height. Andy and Robinson passed to five-ten. Bobby Ray decided he'd enter at six feet. Skeets went in at five-six. He cleared it on his first attempt. He also cleared five-eight. At five-ten, all the decathletes, except Bobby Ray, were in. Or had been in. Three decathletes were out. A boy from Bangor, Maine, who'd won the shot put, failed after leaping five-six. Two others dropped out after making it past five-eight. Still, there were ten decathletes jumping. It looked as if the high jump would last into midafternoon. And it did.

With ten boys inching their way up, the bar rose from five-ten to six feet, to six-two. Then two more decathletes dropped out. At every height, each contestant had three chances. Up until six-two, Skeets breezed through, clearing on his first attempt every time. Andy was having an easy time, too. Another boy having an easy time was Steve O'Grady, the lad from Boston, who was in fourth place. Robinson was struggling, making it on second and third attempts. He complained that his timing was off. But only Bobby Ray, a natural high jumper, was clearing the bar with tremendous margins.

Skeets missed for the first time at six-two. Robinson also missed.

As they sat down together, Robinson said, "I got bad vibes about this height. I can't get my timing down. My steps are off."

When Robinson missed for the second time, Skeets wondered if maybe he was also near the end. But he went up and over on his second try. Andy cleared six-two, as did O'Grady and, of course, Bobby Ray. Robinson willed himself over the crossbar and was ecstatic.

"I'm into no-man's-land," said Andy when the bar was raised to six-four. "I've never gone this high before." Steve O'Grady had joined them. Like Andy, he was extremely fast. He was medium-sized with red hair and freckles. Skeets immediately thought of Becky, and wished she were in the stands cheering him on.

Eight decathletes were still in at six-four. The announcer made a note of it, saying he hadn't seen so many at such a height in the years he'd been at the Eastern States.

As usual, Andy led off. He startled himself by clearing the bar on his first try. He rolled over on the huge blue mats, got to his knees, and shot a triumphant fist into the air. Bobby Ray also cleared, but in less dramatic fashion. He sailed over the bar with ease and inches to spare. He slid off the mats and trotted back to his umbrella. Robinson missed, and walked away shaking his head. Skeets got up, flexed himself, and stood for a moment under the bar. It was seven inches above his head.

From under the umbrella, he heard a familiar snicker. He went to his mark. Turning, he stared at the bar. He rocked back and forth on the balls of his feet. He visualized Mr. MacColl's instructions—his steps, his approach, his arching back, the snapping up of his legs. *Power! Power! Power!* He pranced toward the bar. He planted his foot and sprang upward, twisting in the air in the Fosbury Flop, made famous in the 1968 Olympics by Dick Fosbury, the Oregonian known as the Wizard of Foz. He arched his back. He felt the bar as he barely brushed it. Then, with a hard jerk, he snapped his legs up. His feet just missed the bar. He was over, crashing onto the mats.

Somersaulting off the mat, he raced around wildly, holding both hands in the air. He heard the crowd in Downing Stadium cheering. And the cheers were for him. The smallest decathlete who'd cleared an extraordinary height. *If only Becky were here.* As he danced past the umbrella there was no snicker.

O'Grady and two others also cleared six-four. Robinson missed on his final two attempts. As he slumped next to Skeets and Andy, he said, "There goes my short-lived lead. Nobody'll catch Bobby Ray now."

At six-six, only Bobby Ray made it over—and he did it on his first attempt. All the decathletes then moved away from the high jump pit, except Skeets. He wanted to watch Bobby Ray jump. He marveled at what a wonderful athlete he was. He could do everything, and do it well. He remembered Mr. MacColl's story about the King of Sweden telling Jim Thorpe, after he'd won the decathlon in the 1912 Olympics, that he was the world's greatest athlete.

But Bobby Ray failed at six-eight. He walked up to his umbrella and kicked at it mightily. The umbrella flew up in the air. Like a wounded bird, it wobbled erratically before thumping back to earth near Skeets. It bounced once and landed on his lap. He stood up, holding the umbrella. Instead of coming over to retrieve the umbrella, Bobby Ray grabbed his other gear and stalked off the field. Skeets placed the umbrella back on the ground. He joined Andy, Robinson, and Steve O'Grady on the track near the starting line for the 400 meters, the last event of the first day of the decathlon.

In the first heat of the 400, it was again Andy, Bobby Ray, Robinson, and Skeets. O'Grady was in the second heat. When the first heat drew its lane assignments, Skeets got the outside lane. He'd never run a 400. He didn't know what to expect. Robinson drew the other outside lane. Andy and Bobby Ray had the middle lanes. They knelt in a staggered lineup with Skeets in front and Robinson seemingly far back, awaiting the starter's signal. When it came, they were off, thundering around the first turn.

Skeets didn't know exactly how to pace himself. He didn't want to run out of gas on the final straightaway. He moved gracefully into the back straightaway. He was way out in front, but he knew that when they hit the second turn, the stagger would almost be made up and they'd all be coming abreast of each other.

But Bobby Ray and the speedster, Andy, were on his heels before he started into the back turn. Unable to judge how fast he ought to be running and how much energy he ought to be expending, Skeets found he'd been running too slowly. They caught up to him and moved ahead. Their lead increased as they barreled into the final turn and headed down the home stretch. Robinson was nowhere in sight.

Skeets lengthened his stride. His burst closed the gap. But his chest hurt. His legs felt heavy. He knew he was running out of gas.

He pushed on as hard as ever.

The four runners tore along the last straightaway. Andy was ahead, Bobby Ray a close second. Skeets was right behind him, Robinson further back. And in that order they stumbled across the finish line, gasping, holding their aching sides. Robinson dropped to his knees, panting like a dog.

The times were quickly posted. Andy ran the 400 meters in 52.97 seconds. Bobby Ray made it around the oval in 53.38 seconds. Skeets's time was 53.52 seconds. Robinson, who had died on the second turn, came in at 55 seconds even.

When the points were tallied and posted for the first day, Bobby Ray was in front. He had 3,676 points, well ahead of his pace of a year ago. Robinson was in second with 3,517 points. Andy was third with 3,459 points, followed closely by Steve O'Grady with 3,438. In eighth was Skeets. He had tallied 3,288 points—388 points behind the leader.

23

That evening at the MacColl apartment, the small contingent of athletes from Hackett's Falls gathered happily around the kitchen table. Tommy Patneau had come in fifth in the pole vault, clearing a personal best of fourteen feet three inches. Tomorrow the others would get their chances. Emile McIntosh in the shot put and Billy Abbott in the 110-meter high hurdles. Skeets had an outside chance to place in the decathlon. Even so, he felt down. The shot put foul continued to rankle him. He sat quietly, knowing there was no way he'd catch Bobby Ray. Or anybody. He was too far down in the standings—and Bobby Ray and Robinson and Andy and Steve O'Grady were too good to make fatal mistakes.

Mr. MacColl sensed Skeets's apprehension. "I always loved the second day of the decathlon more than the first," he said. "The events are more technical, harder to do. A lot of times those who do well the first day fade on the second."

"This isn't like Vermont," Skeets said, toying with his dessert spoon. "All the boys down here are good. They're big, and a good big boy'll always beat a good small boy."

"There's more to a good athlete than physical strength," Mr. MacColl said, trying to buck up Skeets. The other boys looked at Mr. MacColl over their dessert plates as he talked. "You've got to have mental toughness. How will a great athlete react in a moment of crisis? I saw how you reacted on top of Catamount Ridge during that awful storm. Remember? I can't help but wonder how Bobby Ray would've reacted if he'd been up there instead of you."

Digging his spoon into the pile of ice cream, Skeets said, "But what kinda crisis can there be in a decathlon? It's only a track meet."

"You never know," Mr. MacColl said. "Every sporting event, every game, every stage in life has its turning point. Even the decathlon has its moment of crisis."

When the Hackett's Falls athletes awoke on Saturday morning, Skeets slipped groggily out of his sleeping bag in the middle of the living room. He stretched and looked at his companions. They stirred one by one. He shuffled to the window. *Today I'm gonna finish my first decathlon. My parents will be proud, I know. And maybe Becky. Maybe.* Peering through the curtains, he noticed that the sidewalk and street were black and glistening with rain. Huge drops splattered down, forming puddles. He looked up and saw the sky, dark with roiling clouds.

"It's pouring out," he said as Mr. MacColl entered the living room. "They won't cancel the meet, will they?"

"Oh, great," groaned Emile. "There goes my chance in the shot put!"

"Hey, a little water never hurt anyone," Mr. MacColl said. "In the kitchen closet, Skeets, there're several umbrellas and a tarp. A little shelter from the rain. Be kind enough and go fetch 'em."

On his way to the closet, Skeets took out Becky's bandanna, smelled her fragrance again, and hid it under his singlet, next to his heart.

After breakfast, they drove across to the East Side of Manhattan in a heavy downpour, got on the FDR Drive, and headed toward Randall's Island. Inside the station wagon, everyone was quiet. In the gloom of Downing Stadium, umbrellas and tarps sprouted everywhere. On the field, officials huddled together. They stared up at the sky. Now and then one of them stuck his hand out from under an umbrella, as if measuring the rain.

Most of the decathletes were already on the field.

Skeets went to join them while Emile headed slowly to the shot put ring, where he knew he'd be competing against forty-two strong-armed kids from all over the place.

Bobby Ray paced back and forth, his umbrella on his shoulder. Robinson knelt on the edge of the track, running a big hand over the wet grass. Steve O'Grady stood still in the rain, his wet hair plastered tightly against his head. Andy Van Buren jogged slowly down the track, turned, and jogged slowly back. As he jogged he twitched his neck and shoulders. Skeets jogged behind Andy. The rain was steady and dispiriting.

Finally, a decision was made. The meet would go on. If it got any worse, it would be canceled.

When the announcement was made, Bobby Ray stopped in his tracks. He looked at one of the officials in disbelief. Turning quickly, he ran into the bleachers to his father. After a bit, the Olympian, Bobby Ray Sr., came down out of the stands. With his son walking behind him like a shadow, they approached the officials. Skeets was impressed by how tall and handsome he was, well over six feet. He had a small paunch, though. Middle age had caught up with him. Still, he was an imposing figure.

"You're not really going to allow this meet to go on?" Bobby Ray Sr. said. "It's dangerous. The track's slippery. The pole vault'll be a disaster! Somebody might get hurt. Postpone it a day."

"We can't, Mr. Barnes," answered an official named Jerry Elliott. His white hair was partly hidden beneath a red baseball cap. "Randall's Island's not available to us tomorrow and there isn't time to find another site."

"Just cancel the meet, then!"

"And let all these kids miss out on the meet of their lives? No sir! We've checked the weather forecast and this is only a passing storm. It'll be gone soon."

"Then wait until it's gone," Bobby Ray Sr. said.

"No sir. We've got to keep to our schedule."

"You and your schedules!"

As he listened to the agitated conversation, Skeets didn't see Mr. MacColl, an umbrella shielding him from the rain, hobble up to Bobby Ray Sr. and the official. Barnes was so much taller than Mr. MacColl, it made Skeets wonder how he'd ever lost to him. Mr. MacColl held out his good hand, feeling the rain.

"You're not afraid of a little water, are you, B.R.?" he said.

Bobby Ray Sr. turned. "MacColl!" he said, recognizing his old nemesis.

The official looked at Mr. MacColl. "You're Billy MacColl, aren't you?" MacColl nodded. "Well, son of a gun. I remember when you used to compete here years ago, while in high school."

"And on days worse than this," Mr. MacColl said. "And I

remember you, Mr. Elliott." He offered his left hand and Elliott shook it.

"My son's right," Bobby Ray Sr. said. "It is you. I'd been told you were killed in some airplane crash in the Vietnam jungles. Glad I was a draft dodger back then. Got me an Olympic silver medal instead of a cheap military Purple Heart."

Elliott's eyes widened and he pressed his lips together. But Mr. MacColl ignored the comment. "I see your son's getting as famous as you," he said. "He certainly looks to be a fine athlete."

"He's better than I was at his age."

"Then he *and you* shouldn't be afraid of a little rain. Besides, B.R., it'll be gone in a few hours."

"We're so far ahead, and with the talent I've seen here, there's no way my son can lose. Even in the rain! But if you think your little pup over there can beat him, well, then we'll be happy to let the meet continue. Too bad the kid isn't your son—we could resume our feud. Your boy against my boy."

With that, Bobby Ray Sr. headed back to the stands while his son and Skeets looked at each other through the rain. A loud clap of thunder roared overhead.

Then Jerry Elliott said to Mr. MacColl, as they watched Bobby Ray Jr. finally trail after his father, "If you hadn't gone in the navy I bet you'd've been in the Olympics instead of Barnes. Why, I remember telling my wife the day you got your commission that it took a lot of guts to give up an Olympic dream to serve your country instead. A lot of guts. Made me proud."

Skeets looked up at Mr. MacColl, his mouth open, eyes wide.

Mr. MacColl glanced at the dark sky. "B.R.'s right," he said. "We best get started."

24

The first heat of the 110-meter high hurdles had Bobby Ray and Andy running on the inside lanes and Robinson and Skeets posted on the outside. Skeets was next to Bobby Ray, an empty lane separating them. Rain dripped off their faces. As they knelt into position, Bobby Ray said to Skeets, "Don't think I'm afraid of a little water. Mathematically, you can't catch me no matter how good you think you are. Besides, my old man said you'd choke just like MacColl always choked when they competed against each other."

Skeets shut his mind to the taunts. He knew in his heart that Mr. MacColl was no choker. He also knew that in his last decathlon he'd beaten Bobby Ray Sr. Then, he couldn't help himself: "At least he didn't choke when it came time to serve his country."

Bobby Ray snorted. "Yeah, whatever."

As the official ordered the hurdlers to get set, Robinson tied a blue bandanna around his head to keep the rain from his eyes. "Rain's the great equalizer," he said.

Bobby Ray shot a surprised look at Robinson. "We'll see," he said.

Seeing that Robinson had tied a bandanna around his head, Skeets slipped Becky's bandanna from under his singlet. Holding it to his nose, he sniffed her fragrance once more, then looped it around his head, knotting it securely in the back.

Bobby Ray snorted. "Whatta we got here? A couple of idiotic Indians?"

Ignoring the slight, Skeets rose into his crouch. His singlet was soaked. Ahead of him puddles shone like ponds on the track. It was a steeplechase instead of a hurdle race. Skeets felt calm—*like the calm before the storm*, he thought, even as it stormed all around him. He believed then that Becky's bandanna was indeed a good-luck charm.

When the gun went off, the four sodden decathletes jerked forward into the rain. All of them were sub-sixteen-second hurdlers, except for Skeets. Andy was probably the fastest. But, as he cleared the first hurdle, he skidded and nearly fell. Miraculously, he regained his balance. Robinson smacked into the third hurdle, splintering it in half. Bobby Ray took each hurdle cleanly, but cautiously. Only Skeets ran with reckless abandon. He loved the rain in his face—the feel of it as it streaked down his arms and legs. Unafraid, he blew by Bobby Ray at the sixth hurdle. He won his heat by almost four-tenths of a second. His time was 15.79 seconds, a remarkable showing in such miserable conditions. Bobby Ray took second with a 16.15. Using the weather as an excuse, he bellyached that it was his worst time in two years.

"On a clear day I'd have blown you away," he said to Skeets. "And you know it."

Andy was third at 16.51, the slip costing him dearly. Robinson never recovered from his collision with the third hurdle and finished at 16.61.

The conditions worsened for the discus. The platter was slippier than soap.

A rattled Bobby Ray complained. "I can't grip this damn thing! It's ridiculous holding a decathlon in these lousy conditions." Standing in the ring, he wiped the discus with a towel as if trying to strangle the life out of it. Tossing the towel aside, he spun quickly. The discus wobbled away. It reminded Skeets of an injured bird. Bobby Ray's best effort in three tosses was 33.80 meters—110 feet 11 inches; he pounded the ground with his fist.

Robinson, big, strong, and glowering with his bandanna shielding his eyes from the rain, uncorked a throw of 37.10 meters—121 feet 9 inches. He jumped out of the back of the ring, clapping his hands; the rain hadn't bothered him. It was the second-best mark of the competition.

Skeets had been taught well by Mr. MacColl. The hard farm life and the hikes to the top of Catamount Ridge made certain he was no ninety-seven-pound weakling. He was solid from head to foot. And even more—he felt at home in the rain. When his last throw was measured, the official called out, "Thirty-five meters point ten. One hundred fifteen feet and two inches."

Entering the pole vault, Skeets was still far behind Bobby Ray. With a score of 4,611, he trailed him by 321 points. Robinson, after his magnificent discus throw, picked up 166 points on Bobby Ray, yet he was down in the dumps. The pole vault frightened him, although he'd cleared ten and a half feet numerous times. Because of the rain the vault terrified him even more.

"When this event's over I'll be so far down in the standings you won't find me," Robinson said to Skeets. "I'll be lucky to clear nine feet."

The decathletes performed their run-throughs—getting their steps down, making sure they got up in the air. It was obvious that Robinson was not alone in his fear of the event. Some of them couldn't even get their poles to bend, trying instead to stiff-pole their way over the bar.

After watching him warm up, Skeets went over to Robinson. He knew that, because of his extraordinary height, speed, and long-jumping ability, he ought to vault a lot higher. One of the hardest things for a vaulter to overcome was the fear of turning upside down. If he could get Robinson to do that, then he might reach another foot or two.

But for the rain.

"You need to rock back," he explained. He showed him what he meant. "Take a shorter run, but run like you're doing the long jump, grip lower on the pole, and turn yourself upside down. Watch how I do it." Skeets made his practice approach, rocked back, and lifted his legs up until they were over his head. The pole bent, held for a second, and lifted him easily into the air. He shot upward like a slingshot. Robinson imitated Skeets. He made five practice jumps. On the fifth, he got upside down.

"Man oh man, that felt great," he said. "I really got upside down for the first time."

Bobby Ray strode past, rain splattering off his face. "You should never teach your opponent how to beat you!"

Robinson and Skeets looked at each other. Then Robinson said, "That white boy sure hates to lose."

The vault started at eight feet. Several vaulters missed on their first try. The more confident vaulters, like Bobby Ray, Skeets, and

117

Steve O'Grady, passed until the bar reached eleven feet. Bobby Ray planned to come in at eleven-six, only because of the rain.

Meanwhile, Robinson felt his heart pumping wildly as he peered down the runway for his first attempt at eight feet. Remembering what Skeets had shown him, he took off. He slammed the pole into the planting box, rocked back, snapped his powerful legs over his head, and sailed high over the bar. He jumped off the mat pointing at Skeets, then pumped his fist back and forth.

The bar was raised to eight-six. Everyone cleared, including Robinson. One of the vaulters dropped out at nine-six, two more at ten feet, and two at ten-six. Andy got over at eleven feet. And so did Steve O'Grady. And to his astonishment, Robinson soared over the bar for his personal best in the event. Skeets also cleared the crossbar.

But one vaulter, Lee Cushman from Richmond, Virginia, in a frightening accident got literally knocked out of the competition because of the rain. His top hand slipped off the wet pole after it had bent. The pole then snapped straight up with sudden force. It slammed into his chest with a loud, terrible thwack that everyone standing nearby heard. Cushman cried out and toppled to the mat. He rolled around as if he'd been shot. An ugly red welt ran from his shoulder down to his thigh. All the decathletes ran to the mat. The official signaled for medical help. It took a half hour before they got him to the bleachers.

"I'm not vaulting anymore," said Robinson, visibly upset. "That could happen to me. To any one of us."

"His hand slipped off the pole," said Steve O'Grady. "That's why it happened."

"Well, I'm still not vaulting. Especially in this rain."

"Come on, Robinson," Skeets said. "I'm staying in and you should, too."

"Yeah," said O'Grady. "I'm in."

"All right, but my heart isn't in it."

Skeets softly punched Robinson on the arm. "That's the spirit. We're all in this together."

At the next height—eleven-six—Bobby Ray entered the competition.

"I wouldn't be going in at such a low height if it wasn't for the rain," he said. "I usually go in at fourteen feet, but after what happened to that stiff from Richmond—Cushman, or whatever his name is—I figured I better get this over with."

Vaulting first, he sprinted down the runway, made his plant, and rocked back with such grace, Skeets had to admit Bobby Ray was a beautiful and talented vaulter. But on his way up he let the pole straighten out too quickly. Before clearing the bar, he bailed out. He slammed the pole hard against the mat, and swore.

Next up, Robinson stood at the top of the runway. Skeets saw he was more nervous than ever. He wanted to shout out encouragement. Yet he kept his mouth shut for fear he'd make Robinson worse off than he now was. Robinson took a deep breath and sprinted down the runway. He planted his pole in the box, swung his thick legs up, and for a second looked as if he was going to bail out. Instead, he popped over the bar.

"I can't believe this!" he said, grinning with such ferocity Skeets thought he'd pull a muscle in his cheek.

Skeets, putting out of his mind the image of Cushman rolling in pain on the mat, had no trouble at eleven-six, and made it on his first attempt. He couldn't help but cast a look of defiance toward Bobby Ray. He felt ashamed after he did it. It wasn't like him to act boastful. His father would've called him on it if he'd seen that look. As it turned out, the look galvanized Bobby Ray. In spite of the rain, he flew over the bar, clearing it by four feet. Skeets had never seen anybody get that high in the air—not even his high school teammate Tommy Patneau. Bobby Ray returned the look of defiance.

At twelve feet, Skeets was again successful. This time, he dared not look Bobby Ray's way. He didn't want to restart a feud. But then, maybe it was too late.

When it was his turn, Bobby Ray raced down the runway, rainwater exploding at his feet. His pole banged into the planting box. But, instead of shooting upward, he slid down the slippery pole in such a way that it reminded Skeets of the time he saw a fireman coming down the pole during a demonstration at the Hackett's Falls fire station.

As Robinson got ready for his attempt, Skeets hollered at him. "You can do it, Robinson! Be more aggressive on your takeoff. Come on, you can do it! I know you can!" Robinson nodded toward him. He no longer thought of Cushman. He sprinted hard toward the pit. His pole bent on impact with the planting box. He went upside down and rode the pole over the bar. *Unbelievable*, he thought, as he descended to the mats below. *Twelve feet!*

Bobby Ray slid down his pole again. The rain was too much of an obstacle for him. And now, with one attempt left, it dawned on him that his first-place standing was in jeopardy. Grabbing a dry towel, he wrapped it tightly around the end of his pole. He carried the pole to the top of the runway. With a deep breath, he dried the pole, tossed the towel away, and ran as fast and hard as he could. He hit the box and rose up and over. But on the way down, his chest brushed the crossbar. It wobbled and for a horrifying moment threatened to tumble off. But it held. Bobby Ray was saved.

"That's it! Too dangerous," he cried, climbing off the soaked mats. He put away his pole and stomped off the field. At twelve-six, Robinson finally missed on all three attempts. The official looked around for Bobby Ray. But the star athlete was in the stands, huddled under an umbrella with his father.

And on a rainy afternoon, in sopping wet Downing Stadium, before teams from all over the East Coast, Skeets soared like an eagle to a personal best of thirteen feet six inches.

At the end of eight events, the standings showed Bobby Ray still in first, but his sizable lead had shrunk. He had scored 5,457 points. Robinson was second with 5,313. Skeets moved into third with 5,262.

With two events to go, the javelin and 1500-meter run, Skeets wondered if he could overcome Bobby Ray's margin of 195 points. In fact, he wondered if he could catch Robinson, ahead of him by 51 points. He looked to be a formidable javelin thrower. Warming up for the javelin, he was told Billy Abbott had placed seventh in the 110-meter high hurdles. It was a great feat because there'd been twenty-eight entrants. He hoped that later in the afternoon Emile would do well in the shot put.

Every time he picked up the aluminum spear, Skeets was amazed by its lightness when compared to his homemade spears cut from saplings. It felt like a feather in his hands. His homemade spears were certainly heavier. He hefted it, amused he could actually throw it as far as he could. But the steady, unending rain was sure to put a damper on everyone's efforts. *Some passing shower*, he thought.

Still, with his body glistening with a mixture of rainwater and sweat, he uncorked a beauty. The javelin sailed 49.12 meters—161 feet 2 inches. Robinson then tossed the javelin farther, with an effort of 51.22 meters—168 feet even. Bobby Ray slid on the grass during his first attempt and fouled.

On his second attempt, Skeets reached only 44 meters. Robinson also fell short of his first effort. Bobby Ray kept his footing and fired the javelin 45.94 meters—150 feet 9 inches. On his last try, Skeets managed to put together all the things Mr. MacColl had taught him, plus what he'd learned on his own atop Catamount Ridge. Soon after the javelin left his hand, it rose quickly, like on a conveyor belt. When it finally pierced the sod, it had traveled 53.84 meters—176 feet 8 inches. It was not even his best throw, yet under such terrible conditions it was a mighty performance.

Robinson shook his head as he got ready for his last attempt. He yelled at Skeets, "Where do you get that power?"

Laughing, Skeets flexed the bicep of his throwing arm.

Robinson did not match his best throw. But he was happy with his first try and happier when Bobby Ray, although not slipping, failed again to get off a decent toss.

The standings had decidedly closed. Bobby Ray's lead was less than 100 points. He held on to the top spot with 5,986 points. Robinson was second with 5,920, and Skeets third with 5,908.

The tired, drenched decathletes now had a thirty-minute wait for the start of the final event, the 1500 meters. The dreaded metric mile!

25

With the rain coming down in sheets, athletes, coaches, and spectators were all miserable. They huddled under tarps and umbrellas. Or took shelter under the eaves. Yet few people complained. In the stands, Mr. MacColl told Skeets he looked rather handsome with Becky's bandanna wrapped about his head, then he toweled the water from Skeets's sopping hair, and off his neck and shoulders.

"This is your event," he said of the 1500. "You've got a chance to win the whole thing if you can run the course in four and a half minutes."

Skeets looked up at Mr. MacColl. "Maybe Bobby Ray's a great miler," he said.

"It looks to me like he's a fair-weather athlete. I heard he's been griping all day about the conditions. I believe you can take him."

"Why do you want me to beat him? It's because of his father, isn't it?"

Mr. MacColl stopped rubbing Skeets's hair with the towel. He tapped the top of his head, a light but scolding tap. "He called you a little pup, didn't he?"

"You told Emile that what counts is just doin' the best you can. But you want me to do more than that."

Mr. MacColl sat down next to Skeets. He put his good arm around him. He was silent for a long time, his arm squeezed tight over Skeets's shoulders. When he finally spoke, there was a catch to his voice.

"It's hard to explain what it was like in the nineteen sixties," he said. "Anti-war demonstrators chanting 'Make love, not war.' I could've joined them, but chose the navy instead and I did my duty. That official down there, Jerry Elliott, was right. I should've been in the Olympics. When I saw Barnes and realized you'd be going up against his son, I forgot that athletics are supposed to be fun. Not to settle old grudges. You're right. It was wrong of me."

122

Mr. MacColl let go of Skeets and gave the top of his head another tap. "I've been blinded by my own personal grudge. That's not fair to you. The feud's between Barnes and myself, not you and his son. So run the fifteen hundred because you love to run—like you were up on Catamount Ridge. Don't run it to settle an old score for me."

Skeets stood and stuck out his left hand. For a moment, Mr. MacColl didn't know what Skeets was doing. Then he realized he wanted to shake his hand. He offered him his left hand.

"Thanks for bein' my coach," Skeets said. He leaned over and quickly embraced Mr. MacColl. Leaving him standing alone, he turned toward the track, suddenly ashamed of the way he'd treated Mr. MacColl when he'd first come to the farm and taken away his room. At that moment the rain stopped and the sun broke through the heavy cover of clouds. Fair weather had returned for the final event.

By the time all twelve decathletes who'd survived the two days of competition reached the start line for the 1500, the track was steaming in the sudden sunlight.

Bobby Ray's mood had changed. He bounced on the balls of his feet, a grin spreading across his handsome face. He knew the only way he'd lose was if Robinson Jesse James beat him by at least ten seconds. He knew Robinson was not a long-distance runner. And the unknown country bumpkin from up north, well, he wasn't even going to think about him.

Skeets still heard Mr. MacColl's voice rattling inside his head. *Run the fifteen hundred because you love to run. Run as if you were up on Catamount Ridge.*

Robinson squinted up at the sun. "My coach says I can win this thing if I run a four-forty. But I've never run a four-forty in my life. I always die during the final lap."

Suddenly, like he'd been struck by lightning left over from the storm, Skeets wanted Robinson to win. At first he'd been intimidated by the big, hulking African American from Philadelphia. But, for two days they'd shared the ups and downs of a decathlon. Now they were friends. An idea flashed in his mind.

"Listen," he said under his breath, like plotting something sinister. "Make believe there's a five-foot rope tied around both our waists," he said. "Yours and mine. Imagine in your mind's eye that the rope is attached to us. Stay that close to me all the way— five feet, like you're being pulled along. You'll win the decathlon."

In a dumbfounded way, Robinson stared at Skeets. "You don't want to win? After all we've been through?"

Skeets didn't know exactly what to say. "Just bein' here's been a thrill," he finally said. "I'm happy enough meeting guys like you and Andy and Steve, guys from all over the East, from places I've never been."

Twelve runners lined up. Missing was Lee Cushman, the injured kid from Virginia.

"Think only of the five-foot rope," Skeets repeated. "Don't let it get taut. Don't let it snap in two. Stay with me!"

The gun barked. The runners broke into an easy trot, jockeying for position on the inside lane. They stayed bunched up around the first turn. Andy Van Buren led the pack, followed by Steve O'Grady, Bobby Ray, Skeets, and Robinson. Robinson fastened his eyes on Skeets's waist. He imagined the five-foot rope, trusting himself to that tough little half-white, half-Indian kid—or whatever mix he was—from the woods of Vermont.

As the pack strung itself out during the first lap, Andy moved ahead by a few meters. But still the order did not change. Each runner waited for the right moment to make his move. Into the second lap, Andy wavered and slipped into second and then third place. O'Grady remained in second as Bobby Ray pulled ahead.

Then O'Grady faltered and fell behind Skeets and Robinson. Around the far turn, Bobby Ray opened up a five-meter lead. Skeets knew his moment had come. A warmth of joy swept through him, from head to foot. Never had he felt so confident. *If only Becky Winslow could see me now!* He put both hands on the bandanna and, turning his head, hollered, "Robinson, remember that five-foot rope. Don't let it snap." Then Skeets quickened his pace dramatically. "Let's go!"

Skeets's feet fell softly on the track. His back and head were now erect. For a moment he thought of Mr. MacColl telling him how Olympian Bill Toomey played mind games with himself at the beginning of each event, imagining he was the strongest thrower in the decathlon, the highest jumper, the swiftest runner. Closing his eyes for a second, Skeets envisioned himself racing over the rocky ledges and fallen logs of Catamount Ridge. He was the elusive mountain lion on the hunt, loping after its prey. And that prey was Bobby Ray.

The crowd immediately sensed a change in the race. A roar went up. A voice from the stands pierced the din, loud and frantic. "Pick it up, Bobby Ray! Pick it up! They're gaining on you!"

Skeets saw every muscle in the back of Bobby Ray's legs, smeared with mud, as he closed in on him. He saw the sweat rolling down his thighs. He saw his neck, red in the sunlight, the rattail hair bouncing back and forth. He heard his hard breathing. He caught up with him and for a moment they ran side by side, stride for stride. Their steps fell together like soldiers on double-quick parade. And in a heartbeat, Skeets slipped past the defending champion, the prep school phenom featured in *Sports Illustrated*.

Bobby Ray could only watch helplessly as his adversary snatched the lead. Gasping, he uttered, "How come I never heard of you?"

Then Robinson passed him. As the African American moved in front, Bobby Ray spat at him. But Robinson never saw him do it. His eyes were riveted to Skeets's waist. The rope was real in his mind's eye. In this eerie, hypnotic state he could see every rough fiber as it pulled him along. The two runners moved in unison around the oval.

In the stands, Emile McIntosh, who'd placed eighth in the shot and felt good about it, said to Mr. MacColl, "It's like those two are tied together by a chain, or something. I'm going down to cheer them on!"

For Skeets, every footfall was perfect, every breath effortless. His arms swung easily. He wanted to close his eyes, but knew if he did he might run off the track. His lead stretched from five to ten meters, to fifteen and twenty. Running down the final straightaway, he opened up a fifty-meter gap on Bobby Ray. Matching him step for step, only five feet away, was Robinson, his eyes never leaving

125

Skeets's narrow waist. As they crossed the finish line, Skeets raised his arms in jubilation.

On the track, Robinson collapsed. His chest heaved. There seemed to be no air left in his lungs.

Bobby Ray puttered the final few meters like an old beat-up car, then slowly ran off the track and into the stands and the consoling arms of his father.

The times showed that Skeets had run the 1500 in 4:32.31. Robinson was right with him at 4:33.54. Bobby Ray's disappointing time was 4:46.40.

After the points were tallied, the announcer blared over the loudspeaker that there had been a major upset in the Eastern States decathlon championship.

"Ladies and gentlemen, in one of the closest, most exciting competitions ever in this hard-fought event, the new champion, with six thousand six hundred and forty points, from Philadelphia's Overbrook High School—Robinson James! Second place, from Hackett's Falls, Vermont, with six thousand six hundred and thirty-eight points—Skeets Stearns! And in third, with six thousand six hundred and twenty-seven points, the defending champion from East Neck, Long Island—Bobby Ray Barnes Jr.!"

Robinson threw his arms around Skeets. "That was the shortest rope I ever saw in my life!" He was panting. "And you want to know something? I'm going to dream about that imaginary rope for a very long time." He dropped his hands to his sides, still panting. "Without that rope I'd never have won. You may come from a small town, but let me tell you, you've got a heart as big as all Philadelphia. And you know what? I want you to come down to my City of Brotherly Love someday, let me show you around my neighborhood."

"And Robinson," Skeets said between deep breaths, "you gotta make a trip up to New England and see my Green Mountains of Vermont. Indian territory. I gotta secret swimmin' hole that'll blow you away."

"Deal," Robinson said.

The new friends then high-fived and went their separate ways.

Waiting at the side of the track, Skeets spotted Emile. With a broad smile, the Big Apple grabbed him in a headlock. Instead of a noogie, he flipped Skeets up onto his broad shoulders and carried him triumphantly around the track.

"We did okay," Emile hollered up to him, "for a couple of local yokels from the sticks."

"Yeah," said a flushed, beaming Skeets, "we sure did!"

Epilogue

The school year was almost over. Summer was near. In a few days the corn crop would be planted and the first cutting of hay done on the Stearns farm. There'd be plenty of chores to do. But the best part for Skeets—he and Becky were training together for the Vermont State High School Multi-Event Championships.

Since coming back from the championship in New York City, he'd taken her out once for a pizza. Over spicy slices slathered with cheese, tomatoes, pepperoni, and mushrooms, they first discussed competing together in the multi-event championships to be held down at Middlebury College.

"When I heard about the decathlon, competing in all those events," Becky said over her slice of pizza, looking him straight in the eye, "I checked into a similar thing for girls. I found out about the heptathlon. And guess what? This year, for the first time, the state will hold a championship for it along with the decathlon. I want to do it!"

"I haven't heard of the heptathlon." Skeets took a bite of his pizza, keeping his eyes on Becky and admiring her pretty face crowned by red hair.

"It's new," she said. "There used to be the five-event pentathlon for women. Now two more events have been added."

"What are they? I wonder if Mr. MacColl knows anything about the heptathlon."

"The events are the hundred, I've done that—I should have beaten that Canadian gal; the high jump, done that, too; the shot put, not done that; the two hundred and long jump—along with the hundred, my specialties; the javelin, new for me; and the eight hundred. I know I can run the eight hundred. Twice around the track."

"No pole vault?" They laughed.

"Not yet," Becky said. "That'd make it an octathlon." They laughed again. They finished their pizza.

"Then let's train together for the states," Skeets said hopefully. Becky nodded.

They'd work hard. It wouldn't be a date, she told him. They'd keep their training strictly business.

Now all he had to do was dig up enough courage to ask her to the junior prom. Training was one thing. Going out on a date was another.

Meanwhile, between training and waffling back and forth about asking her to the prom, up on Catamount Ridge when his chores were done, he and Mr. MacColl enjoyed their Sunday afternoons swimming in the mountain pool.

Mr. MacColl's fear of the forest was gone. On occasion he hiked up the ridge by himself. The water's buoyancy made him feel whole. When he swam, the old wounds seemed as if they were not there. In the cold water he believed he was young again. He never wanted to leave this place. Yet he knew the day was coming soon when he'd go back to New York, close up his mother's apartment, and get on with his life. He sat at the edge of the pool. Nearby, Skeets leaned on a boulder, sunning himself.

"I hear from Emile that you've been seeing a lot of this Becky girl these days," Mr. MacColl said. "Emile said the two of you are training for the multi-event championships. I think that's great. Anything else going on?"

"No," Skeets said, blushing. "We talk some. I took her out for a pizza once. That's about it."

"She's quite pretty. Isn't the junior prom coming up soon?"

Skeets nodded. *How'd he know all this stuff, and how'd he know I wanted to take her to the prom?*

"She reminds me some of my old girlfriend, Kathleen Fleming."

Skeets knew how Kathleen had dumped him after he'd been wounded. He hurriedly picked up a stone and chucked it as far as he could. Neither of them spoke for a while.

Finally, Mr. MacColl broke the silence. "The last event of the decathlon—it seems I never really asked you about the fifteen hundred."

They'd talked a lot about the decathlon, analyzing each event. But the fifteen hundred had never been fully discussed.

"You had a chance to win the decathlon, but you chose to let someone else claim that glory. Why? It belonged to you."

Picking up another stone, Skeets hurled it across the pool. "I dunno," he said. "I've thought about it, but I can only remember what I felt at that moment. I was in this trance."

He bent down and selected yet another stone, this time a perfectly round one. He felt its smoothness, like velvet in his hand. Straightening up, he went on, "I knew then I was going to win. Don't ask me how I knew. I just knew. And I wanted to share that feeling with someone. There was no one there I wanted to share it with as much as Robinson James. When he won, I felt as if I'd won, too."

"Kind of a Zen thing, huh?" Mr. MacColl said. "It's not the goal that counts, but the doing."

"I guess," Skeets said. "Yeah, that's the way I feel." He then fired the smooth, round stone across the pool. "Besides, I got the states in a week at Middlebury and then the Easterns next year." He watched the stone skip over the water. It clattered against the far cliff. Rattling around for a second or two, it bounced backward and into the water.

"I used to feel like that myself, a long time ago," Mr. MacColl said. "The guy who founded the modern Olympic Games one hundred years ago, a Frenchman, Pierre de Coubertin, felt the same way. He had this motto I lived by until I got hurt. Then I forgot it. I tossed it away just like you tossed that stone. To put it simply, de Coubertin said the most important thing in life is not the triumph, but the struggle. The essential thing, he said, is not to conquer, but to fight well. That used to be the Olympic spirit. I guess the way athletes are today, they've all forgotten that guiding spirit."

"Like Bobby Ray Barnes," Skeets said. He saw, in his mind's eye, Bobby Ray running up into the bleachers and into the arms of his father.

"Like Bobby Ray Barnes," Mr. MacColl said. "Like father, like son. They blamed the loss on the weather. Used it as an excuse.

130

Well, in life there are no excuses. You take what's dealt you, make the best of it, and move on."

"No excuses," Skeets said.

"So, are you ever going to ask Becky Winslow out again, and not just for pizza? Maybe take her to the junior prom?"

"Maybe."

"Maybe? Come on, Skeets. No excuses."

Skeets had to laugh then. So did Mr. MacColl. And Skeets knew at that moment, he would ask Becky to the prom. After all, although he kept it hidden from her, he had Becky's green and gold bandanna that still carried her special fragrance. And that meant so much to him.

High above them, the sun dipped behind the scraggly pines that grew in gnarly shapes on the summit of Catamount Ridge. The afternoon shadows lengthened. It was time to head home. As they got up, Skeets sensed something in the shadows. Mr. MacColl limped ahead, moving down the mountain. The skin on Skeets's neck tingled. Turning quickly, he looked along the top of the ridge. The sun was almost down, and it would be dark soon.

There, outlined against the sky in that last glow of sunlight, Skeets saw the mountain lion. It stood silently, head held high, looking down at him. And then, swiftly, the tawny animal slipped over the ridge, and was gone.

The End

Stephen L. Harris is the author of the award-winning trilogy about New York City's National Guard regiments in World War One, including *Duffy's War*, named by the World War One Historical Association as one of the best books ever written about America's participation in the war. The other books in the trilogy are *Duty, Honor, Privilege* and *Harlem's Hell Fighters*, praised by documentary film producer Ken Burns. He also wrote *Rock of the Marne: The American*

Soldiers Who Turned the Tide Against the Kaiser in World War I. According to author and historian Thomas Fleming: "No one writes about World War I with more empathy and understanding than Stephen Harris."

Before working on his World War I books, Steve edited General Electric's corporate magazine, *Monogram*, and in 1996 wrote *100 Golden Olympians* for the US Olympic Committee, a book that honored America's greatest living gold medalists as part of the Modern Olympic Games' 100th anniversary. He was the senior writer on a CD-Rom history of the Olympics, *Olympic Gold*, published by SEA Multimedia of Tel Aviv, Israel. *Olympic Gold* won the 1996 Cannes Film Festival's "Oscar," the Gold Milia d'Or, for world's best reference title.

Today he is the American editor of the *Journal of Olympic History*, the official publication of the International Society of Olympic Historians. The Society awarded its prestigious 2016 Vikelas Plaque to Steve for his many contributions to Olympic history.

Steve also contributed to the *African American National Biography*, edited by Louis Gates, Jr., published by Harvard University Press in 2007. He wrote biographies of prominent soldiers of the 369th Infantry Regiment—Harlem's Hell Fighters.

Steve lives in Middlebury, Vermont, with his wife, Sue.